the Deviant SON

Edith Baranyay

◆ FriesenPress

One Printers Way
Altona, MB R0G 0B0
Canada

www.friesenpress.com

ISBN
978-1-03-913039-5 (Hardcover)
978-1-03-913038-8 (Paperback)
978-1-03-913040-1 (eBook)

1. FICTION, MAGICAL REALISM

Distributed to the trade by The Ingram Book Company

CHAPTER ONE:
Return to Planet Earth

Overwhelmed with anger and frustration
I totally lose control and
get pulled into a fast downward spiral
Slowly the foggy grey area
I had been stuck in begins to dissolve
An eerie calmness follows
Glimpses of pleasant moments in my
former life flash by me
When contentment filled my heart
In this positive mood
I feel courageous, strong, and capable
of handling travesties
Fueled by strong desire to redeem myself
on this peculiar journey...

Suddenly I was jerked about and violently sucked into a dark, confining space. The lightness I had felt before was replaced by a heavy, lumpy weight upon me. Panic took hold when I realized I was underwater. My arms flailed as I tried to escape to the surface. The downward surge was strong and the pain in my chest increased as my lungs struggled for air. An ice-cold force pushed me farther and farther below.

What happened to me? This is not how Max had described his visits to Earth. I feel trapped, stuck in a heavy shell, unable to move. My mind is foggy. Far, far away, Max's voice still echoes: *Focus, Joseph, focus.*

I faintly recall a downward spiral into a pleasant atmosphere, then fear, darkness, cold water, and gasping for breath. Now I'm stuck in a sleep-like stage. If I focus I can lift my right eyelid a tiny bit, just enough to see a sliver of light. The brightness triggers an automatic reflex and the eyelid drops again.

When I'm not in a half-delirious/half-sleeping mode, I can detect faint noises, strange sounds I don't quite recognize. If I'm able to hear, I must be alive. Instinct tells me I'm stuck in a human body. Why can't I get my spirit to connect with its brain, to move my arms and legs? If I landed in a corpse, my brain would not function. It can't be another grey sphere either or I would be able to communicate with other spirits.

I'm sure this is Earth. I noticed blue sky before I hit the water. At one point I catch a glimpse of a semi-dark, bluish space and small, blinking lights. Another glance lets me recognize machines and equipment. That must be where the humming and peeping noises originate.

As I gain consciousness again, I can hear muffled voices. Suddenly a young lad's angry yell comes through clearly: "How can he do that! How can he do that to me? I hate him, hate him, hate him."

Running footsteps from the hall enter the room and several adult voices try to hush the screamer. The conversation fades as they walk out the door. Quiet returns. Before I can collect my thoughts, I hear the click of high heels approaching my bed. Loud screeching attacks my sore brain. "You bloody idiot, what the hell did you jump off of the bridge for? Haven't you caused enough trouble and shame to your poor family already? Who will look after Lucas? How can you do this to your own son?"

A second voice comes through, telling her to calm down. Then the conversation becomes unintelligible as they walk away. My mind is struggling to make sense of what I have learned in the last few minutes.

Vaguely, as if from a great distance, I recall a grey fog. I'm falling. The echo of a voice is trailing behind me. "Focus, focus, Joseph. Focus."

Then I entered a space of lightness before I was sucked into deep water.

Did I crash into this human body?

Am I now trapped in a corpse?

How can that be if I can hear voices?

Who was that screeching woman and how old am I if I am the parent of a child?

What do I look like—am I a man or a woman?

How bad is the damage from the drowning and why can't I move my limbs?

The dullness in my head is slowly being overshadowed by stabbing pain. It comes in waves, reaching its summit when the medications wear off, I assume. During my periods of consciousness I can catch snatches of conversations in the room, though it is not enough information to give me an understanding of who I am and what my physical condition is.

At one point a nurse or doctor hovers over me. Then my right eyelid is lifted and a loud female voice says in the tone of a teacher talking to an errant pupil, "Hey, Mr. Griler, time to wake up from your induced coma. Come on, give me a sign, can you hear me?"

An effort to open my mouth and say how do you know my name fails badly, but I must have managed a tiny grunt because I hear a snicker. A male voice condescendingly chimes in. "Well, well, are we finally coming back? Disappointed you didn't succeed in killing yourself? Wait until your family arrives; they might just finish the job."

My mind is stuck on what the nurse called me.

Griler is my family name.

I know that I died in 1989 and my daughter Liz, who I met in the grey area, told me that my wife and my son Hubert passed away before her. That means there is not much of my family left other than my son Wolfgang, my grandsons, maybe some of my Austrian cousins' descendants.

No matter how hard I try, I can't remember the names of the two grandsons born after my death. I should have paid better attention to what Max told me about his earthly visit.

A female voice whispers close to my face. "I'm sorry. That was totally unprofessional of the doctor to say to a patient. Dr. Weber thinks that, because he is your ex-wife's husband, he has special privileges to vent his anger. In the cafeteria he blabs on and on about how difficult it is for him to deal with your son Lucas. The boy has been acting out violently ever since you jumped off the Penny Bridge."

The Penny Bridge, really? The previous owner of this body jumped off the Penny Bridge? During my lifetime I walked across that antique bridge with the beautifully carved iron railings numerous times. On both sides are donation boxes with a small sign asking for a penny per crossing. The fee is ignored now, but in the nineteenth century, a penny provided a bed for a homeless person. Looks like I'm in Passau.

Good, at least I know where I am and that I'm a man, or I wouldn't have an ex-wife. If only I could talk. Sounds easy, but what would I say? How can I explain that I'm not the person who committed suicide?

I'm afraid this is Wolfgang's body. What would have driven my youngest son to such drastic measures, especially with a child depending on him? Why did nobody from my hometown come for a visit? Where are the neighbors, priest, family doctor?

Liz did say that Wolfgang most likely will lose the family homestead in the divorce from his third wife. Looks like her intuition was spot on. What else did he do to make his ex-wife hate him so? How old is his boy now? He must be at least fourteen, maybe even older. No wonder the child is angry if he has lived with his father for so many years and can't get along with his stepfather. How can a man desert his only child? He didn't just leave town, he decided to drop out permanently. Poor boy!

Below the Penny Bridge the current is quite strong, which explains the powerful downward surge I felt, but how did the body end up in this hospital bed? Did my spirit take over and revive Wolfgang's body?

This hospital room reminds me of science fiction films in the eighties. I'm hooked up to several computerized machines and the room looks super sterile, all white and gleaming.

In a flashback to the grey area, I remember telling Max that I would like to see planet Earth in the twenty-first century, especially the computers he raved about. How ironic—now I'm most likely being kept alive by humming and blinking machines. That's not the way I had imagined my visit to Earth.

The oxygen mask and the tubes attached to my upper body tie me down. Any attempt to move my head seems to be impossible. At one point I thought I felt a little twitch where I imagined my foot might be. My foot? Well, it *is* my foot now, I guess.

How long was I asleep? Is it day time, night time? Must be night because it is so quiet. I'm a bit afraid of what the morning shall bring. Will I have visitors? Are they going to yell at me again? What will I be accused of? Well, what will the person, who used to inhibit this body, be accused of next? I'm afraid I'll find out soon enough.

A friendly voice interrupts my musings. "Good morning, Mr. Griler. Can you open your eyes, can you attempt a smile? We would love to see a little sign from you that you can understand what I'm saying. You have had a traumatic, frightening experience and we are afraid there might be extensive brain damage. Your medications have been changed and you should be coming out of the induced coma today. Any sound or movement from you would give us an idea how this case will proceed. Can you try to open your eyes, just a little bit?"

My first thought is *no way*. I'm not going to help you until I'm sure whose body I'm occupying. Then I change my mind because I realize that I have no choice but to accept my fate and make the best of this crazy situation. I remember Max's last word and focus on opening my eyes. Facing whatever comes my way is my only option.

The friendly voice turns out to be that of a pretty, thirty-something nurse, who exclaims. "Well, well. We are back, aren't we? Good for you. Now follow my finger with your eyes. First left, then right. Well done. Now move your eyes to the left if your pain is tolerable, to your right if it is unbearable. Good, now let's do this again to make sure we got it right. Wonderful, I'll go find the doctor and give him the good news."

Fortunately this doctor, who seems to be near retirement age, has no angry feelings toward me. He detaches a clipboard from the end of my bed and makes notes after studying the numbers on the computer displays. In between writing, he discusses my heartbeat, blood pressure, and physical injuries with the nurse. Before they have a chance to decide which medications might stabilize me and what would work best to help rehabilitate me as fast as possible, there is a knock on the door.

From the way the male who enters the room addresses the doctor and holds up an identification card, I assume he is a policeman. My guess seems to be correct as I hear the doctor explain that the patient is not ready for questioning. In a few days they might have a better idea how badly both mind and body were affected by the suicide attempt.

Before the policeman leaves he turns toward me and says, looking straight in my face, "You are not going to get away from me. I'll make darn sure you pay for all the pain and harm you have caused. Just you wait!"

There we go, another person who hates my guts. Shouldn't a policeman be more professional, less biased? He sounded like he has a personal grievance against me. Well, against whoever occupied this body before me, that is. Speaking of the body, what if there is so much physical damage that I end up in a wheelchair?

Oh no, I can't live that misery again. Two decades with multiple sclerosis is enough pain for one human soul to suffer. If there is a criminal act involved I want to face the judge standing on my own two feet.

Max and I thought we were in limbo because of unresolved issues on Earth. Now it looks like I will be cleaning up a family member's mess. Would be nice to know at least whose misdeeds I will be paying for in exchange for this damaged body.

I have never felt so alone and worried in my whole life. Even in my most miserable moments there were people who cared for me—at times reluctantly, but they always looked after me.

All I know at this point is that the previous occupant of this body used to live with his young son. Where they resided and how they managed is another question. Did he care for the boy, was he a good father?

Before she left, the nurse took blood samples and exchanged the intravenous fluid bags. Since then I have been waiting for improvements, a twinge of nerve pain or a spasm, anything that will prove my vital organs are beginning to function again.

My mind is still fighting the pervading fog, the throbbing pain has lessened, my mouth feels dry and my nose is numb from the tubes the nurse inserted. Slowly, I open one eye and scan the room.

Out of nowhere, a doctor—I suspect he is the one who is married to the ex-wife—appears at my bedside holding a little hammer. With a big grin on his face he starts hitting my legs like a maniac. What on earth is he doing? Is he trying to break my legs? Just as suddenly as he came in he stops and leaves the room. What a nutcase. The ex-wife sure knows how to pick them.

Frantically, I try to move my mouth and my tongue to produce a sound, anything that might resemble a word. In the process I kind of pass out.

As I wake up I can hear several voices in the room. Two have strong Austrian accents and seem to dominate the conversation. A High German-speaking female interrupts their diatribe with an inquiry about the patient's condition and Lucas's whereabouts. Keeping my eyes closed gives me a chance to figure out who they are. Knowing their identity might help me when they confront me with accusations and grievances.

The Austrian female turns out to be the ex-wife. She laments theatrically, "Lucas has run away. I have tried to call Doris but she is not answering the phone. This is her brother, he is her responsibility. She should be looking after him and cleaning up his mess. Lucas needs her, too. Helga, maybe if you call her she will listen to you."

Now we are getting somewhere. Helga is my wife's sister, Doris is my daughter, and I'm stuck in Wolfgang's body. The ex-wife goes on about Wolfgang's trouble with addiction and mental illness until Helga chimes in. "Well, Agnes, you can spare us the details of your unhappy relationship with my nephew. The two of you drove my poor sister to despair. You are no angel, Agnes. Ruthlessly, you took him for every last penny. Lucas is your responsibility, not Doris's. Neither is Wolfgang. Your greed made him lose his home and your relentless badmouthing cost him the goodwill of the neighbors."

"How dare you talk like this to my poor wife. Come, Agnes, let's get out of here. This whole family is totally nuts!" shouts Dr. Eichner.

"Yes, please take your **silly goose** home. She is no use here to anyone."

Agnes mutters **stupid cow** as she passes by my bed.

An unknown male voice says, "I swear I saw our patient's lips twitch for a second. I think he was trying to smile. Looks like he enjoyed this exchange of old-fashioned insults. Did a spark of humor survive in spite of his serious condition and slimy past?"

What a friendly voice—sounds like a sensible man. Could this be Helga's new boyfriend, the one Max was telling me about? The one who comforted Helga when my wife suffered the aneurysm and spent months at the hospital and then in rehabilitation? Hopefully he will be a positive and supportive presence when I have to deal with Wolfgang's problems.

The following prolonged silence makes me nervous. What are they doing now? Are they standing beside my bed and waiting for me to make a move? Should I open my eyes and give them a sign that I'm able to hear and understand conversations?

One of them walks across the room. I hear a chair scraping the floor, then another. Looks like they have settled down and are now quietly discussing what will be their next move.

Should they go home and come back in a few days?

Would they be able to find Lucas?

Do they want to get involved in Wolfgang's disastrous private life?

They decide to wait until the doctor arrives and then call Doris with the latest medical prognosis.

To my delight, I hear the nice senior doctor's voice. After introductions and a friendly greeting, he explains to my visitors that he is concerned over the lack of response from me. There has been little progress other than some eye movement and small facial twitches. He hopes to have a better understanding of my condition in a few days. Helga's friend asks a few questions about the physical damage from the drowning and explains that Wolfgang has acted strangely for years. The family suspected mental issues—at the least, a deep depression.

I understand the depression part because my wife struggled with intense dark periods throughout her life. Addiction had been a problem since Wolfgang's teenage years. The two of us went through horrible fights about his alcohol and drug abuse. For unexplained reasons, I always understood his drinking was not just a matter of party-ing with his buddies, but an attempt to drown out painful memories, insecurities, frustrations—maybe a combina-tion of all of those emotions.

His first wife couldn't handle his drunken episodes and soon grew tired of waiting for him to get his act together.

After the doctor leaves, Helga approaches my bed and speaks thoughtfully. "You know, Wolfgang, for my sister's sake I wish I could help you. All your adult life she pro-tected you, paid your debts, hushed the neighbors, and made excuses for your stupid and senseless behavior. Doris tried too, stubbornly defending you, her little brother. Now with all those accusations against you surfacing, she is deeply hurt and disturbed. She told me that she is not able to face you until she knows all the evidence, hears all the allegations against you, especially the ones made by family members."

Her friend agrees. "At this point, there is nothing we can do for you. This is like an avalanche of all your bad choices and misdeeds hitting you. After getting away so many times, you finally have to face judgment and, since you insulted and pushed away all your family and friends, there is nobody willing to speak up for you and support you. Helga and I will be bystanders. We'll keep an eye on your situation and then report what is happening to Doris."

"This may be the last time we come to visit but we will be in contact with your doctors. Once Doris has worked through her anger and disappointment with you, she may want to speak to you again. That is, if you are ever able to recover your voice.

Wolfgang, you used to be such an adorable baby, what on earth happened to you! You have totally destroyed your life and your child's future. I'm so glad, Erna, your poor mother is no longer alive. It would have killed her to witness such disgrace."

Her last words were barely finished when she started sobbing. Her friend talks to her gently, tries to calm her down.

Then, as they are leaving, they both say almost in unison, "Goodbye, Wolfgang."

Now, as there is no movement in the room, I open my eyes and take in the atmosphere. Today I can see much clearer. The curtains are open and the corner of an apartment block across the street is visible. From the square windows I can tell that it dates back to the early fifties, when architecture went out the window and everything was built as economically and quickly as possible. Since I can't hear any traffic, the hospital must be located in a quiet area; maybe I'm in the General Hospital on the hillside.

Footsteps are approaching and I close my eyes just in case it is Dr. Eichner. Whoever it is enters quietly without a greeting and doesn't make any sound other than a distant kind of beeping off and on. Curiosity overcomes me and I take a peek. A teenage boy is sitting on one of the two chairs in the room and playing around with a small gadget. He looks up and catches me staring at him.

Still holding his toy he comes closer, but never takes his eyes off me. Suddenly, he puts his gadget in front of my face and says cynically, "Smile, Papa, this may be my last photo of you. I'm still mad at you. I came by to tell you that I'm fine. Remember Ahmed? His family is taking care of me.

"You are staring at me like you never saw me before. That's freaking me out. Close your eyes if you can understand what I'm saying. You do? Man, rad. Can you say my name? No, that's OK. Listen, I'm going to school again and I'm studying hard with Ahmed to pass the finals. No more messing around for me. Don't want to end up like you. I'll drop in again in a few days. Maybe you can say something then. Bye."

Cool kid, as my daughter Liz would say. Wolfgang does not deserve such a sensible son. He obviously dealt with a lot of his father's problems before. This suicide attempt seems to have scared him enough to pull up his socks and think about his own future. I'm greatly relieved to know his friend's family is taking care of my grandson. I was worried he would end up homeless, since I have no idea whether they had a home and what their financial circumstances were.

At one time, Wolfgang had a good position with the local government and should therefore be collecting a private pension. Well, that depends on what year it is, how long he worked and what the retirement age is in this new century.

If only I could look in a mirror to see what I look like. This is pure curiosity.

Soon, it starts getting dark outside. A different nurse comes in, closes the curtains, checks the data on the screens, and carries on a distracted monologue as she changes the bags and the catheter. Since she does not seem to care one way or the other, I keep my eyes open and watch her movements until she has completed her tasks. For a moment she stops, looks at me, and says, "Good night, Mr. Griler," before she leaves the room.

The dim nightlight gives me a better view of the screens and, out of boredom, I start studying the numbers. My eyesight seems to be very good—no glasses needed, even in the semi-dark. The lines with the beeping arrows must be my pulse. On the bottom the numbers stay the same and they look like a date **21-02-2017**. That means, since I'm in Wolfgang's body, I'm sixty-one years old.

CHAPTER TWO:
Family Connections

AFTER A LONG NIGHT of alternating between dozing off and staring at the numbers on the screen, I'm looking forwards to seeing a human face—hopefully a friendly one. The nurse who comes in the morning is a different one from the ones I saw yesterday. She notices my open eyes and speaks directly to me, "Good morning, Mr. Griler, how are we today? My name is Theresa. I'll get you all tidied up and ready for the doctor. Then I have to give you an injection because you are scheduled for several tests—among them, a brain scan."

Once she completes all the required procedures, she calls two orderlies to put me on a stretcher and wheel me to the radiation department. The bright lights in the hallways hurt my eyes for a moment. Once my blurry vision clears, I'm amazed how different the people I see walking past me look—the strange hairdos, the clownish amount of make-up, and an amazing mix of fashion styles and accessories. The ride in the elevator is so smooth I can barely tell if we are moving up or down. What a change from the clunky equipment I remember.

We go down another hallway, stop at a door with the warning signs **Authorized Personnel Only. Do Not Enter. Press the Red Button**. Next I'm wheeled toward a huge, white, tube-like machine and put on an examination table. A masked technician in a light blue coat explains that they will be performing a scan of my head and neck. He says to no one in particular, "I hope this low dose of sedation is effective and he won't be able to move. I'll adjust the setting so he won't breathe while he is in the tunnel."

As they push me into the machine I can hear loud humming and see flashes of light. Within seconds, the noise stops and I'm pulled out again, transferred to the stretcher and wheeled down another hallway. The sign above the next door says "Laboratory," and, as my sedation starts to wear off, I'm more aware of the action around me. At one point I think I even blinked as the nurse inserted a needle into my arm to draw blood. She looks at me a bit surprised and then wonders, "Did you actually notice this poke?"

Her voice is so friendly, I feel obligated to make an effort to communicate to her that I can understand her. I manage a small movement with my tongue and a hoarse little grunt. Encouraged by her grin, I try one more time and this time I produce a little noise sounding like "Hello." She laughs, "Well, well, nice effort. Keep it going."

As the orderlies push me back to my room one of them stares at me and remarks, "The world would be better off if you had succeeded with your suicide attempt. From what Dr. Eichner is saying you'll spend the rest of your life in jail anyway. What's the use of recovering? You still have to face all your shit in court."

The other orderly looks a bit embarrassed and tells him, "Just do your job. This is none of your business. He may repent and try to atone for his sins. Leave him be, will you?"

This moment is probably a good sample of what my future will be like, harassed by the righteous and protected from undue punishment by the kind people I will meet. At this point it looks like I will be without support from relatives and friends.

Back in my hospital room I keep musing about my situation. There really is not much family left beside Lucas, Helga, and her kids.

Though Erna and I babysat our nephews and nieces every summer when they were school age, I can't count on support from them if Wolfgang has done either one of them any kind of harm.

If this is really the year 2017, most friends of my generation are probably dead or in pretty bad physical shape. Helga seems to be the exception. She sounded exactly like I remember her. Hannah, my oldest son's widow, and Wolfgang never got along because of her feminist ideals. The grandson, who was born the year I died, is probably busy with a family of his own. The rest of my relatives are third and fourth cousins; none would remember me.

This leaves me to consider the Canadian branch, my oldest daughter Doris's family. What has Wolfgang done to make her so upset that she won't speak to him anymore? I hope Helga can convince her to contact me or Lucas, to give me a chance to talk to her. But then, what would I say? She avoided me like the plague in the last decade of my life. The one time she did come home for a visit, she could barely look me in the eyes and disappeared as soon as I tried to have a conversation with her. It does not really matter who occupies this body, Wolfgang or I—she hates both of us.

At that moment, Dr. Eichner, the idiot husband of Agnes, appears at my bedside, pushes a few buttons on the equipment, and turns around to glare at me. Suddenly, I'm gasping for air. Just as I am about to pass out, he hits a few keys on the computer and I can breathe again. As I try to gain composure he whispers in my ear, "I'm in control now and I'll make you suffer. I'll pay you back for what you have done. Your life will be hell, believe me. You will wish you were dead."

Of course I'm scared to death but I can also feel anger growing deep inside me and a strong need to express my fear, to get out a word, to form a sentence, to communicate to a person in authority what this Eichner is doing to me. Frantically, I look around, hoping that a nurse or another doctor, even a policeman will enter the room and put an end to Eichner's stupid game. Help comes from an unexpected source. "Aren't you Eichner, the husband of Wolfgang's ex-wife? What are you doing here?"

"Ah, Miss Meindl, the holy spinster of our hospital. What a surprise. How on earth do you know my wife?"

The elderly lady looks a bit frail but when she speaks her voice is strong and confident. "Of course I know Agnes. I used to visit Wolfgang's mother every week as long as she lived. Even though she shared the house with her son and his family, she was often alone and had no one to talk to."

"Well, Miss Goody-Two-Shoes, enjoy your visit with the village idiot and child molester. He will be in prison before you can save his soul."

He gives me the finger before he leaves the room. I'm seething in anger and shock. Wolfgang was a child molester? Oh, my Lord, help me. How did this happen? The machine starts beeping wildly and a nurse comes running and adjusts the equipment. She turns to my visitor and chides her for upsetting me.

Miss Meindl calmly corrects her that it was not her but Dr. Eichner who insulted this patient. Then she asks about my condition and if it would be all right if she sat down and read to me from the local paper. The nurse nods and exits the room. Miss Meindl adjusts a chair and starts reading an article on the first page.

"A six-year-old cat named Diablo was tortured and left to die in the street. Luckily, a young man found the injured pet and brought it to the veterinary clinic. Anyone with information regarding this crime should contact the animal protection agency. A reward of 500 Euros will be paid for tips leading to the capture of the criminal… What a sad story, I'll try to find a lighter subject.

"Ah, here is something. The fire department in Hochdorf held their annual sled racing competition. This year, twenty-seven teams took part in the 500-meter race—four mixed teams and two all-women teams were involved for the first time. Look, here is the picture of the winning team."

Miss Meindl really is a sweetheart and takes her volunteer role at the hospital seriously. Among other things I learned that tomorrow will be a sunny day, almost 10 C, but foggy in the Alps. A forty-year-old drunk driver tried to escape the police by driving into a farmer's field and got stuck in the sludge caused by melting snow and warm weather. The oldest Bavarian citizen celebrated her 103rd birthday and 50,000 Romanians protested in Bucharest against their corrupted government. The film **La-La Land** won numerous awards at the British film festival.

Interesting, the oldest Bavarian citizen was born a month before me and, if I had not died in 1989, I would now be the oldest citizen in this state. Miss Meindl must be in her eighties. I know she was born in the thirties, before her father got involved in politics. Her mother was a real lady, raised five kids by herself while the husband was in prison for war crimes and afterward, while he wasted his life as the village drunk.

The oldest boy owned one of those three-wheeled cars. He regularly cruised around in a drunken stupor. Once, when the Austrian border guards did not open the barriers fast enough, he drove right through them, leaving splintered wood behind.

Why did nobody stop him? Because it was the fifties and there were not many cars around at the time. The Americans were in control and did not seem to care if drunk German drivers killed their fellow citizens.

Miss Meindl worked as a teacher at the local middle school. There was a rumor that she wanted to be a nun, but was found unsuitable due to a nervous condition. In my opinion, it was more likely because of her father's Nazi history. This woman does not have a mean bone in her body.

In spite of her advanced age, she sits on the chair gracefully as she reads me the news in her pleasant voice. "The carnival parade on Sunday afternoon was a great success. All big businesses in town participated with fancy floats and free samples for the crowd. The town center was closed all afternoon to accommodate more than a thousand masked and dressed-up citizens of all ages, celebrating the first day of carnival, 2017. The newly elected prince and princess wore traditional costumes. As the mayor handed them the key to the city hall, the crowd cheered wildly."

When the doctor comes in, Miss Meindl exchanges greetings with him and then excuses herself after turning to me and promising to come back as soon as she can. This is a different doctor, and he looks very serious as he tells me that there is a severely damaged section of my brain that will need surgery. The specialist and radiologist have prepared a report. Any further treatment will have to be approved by the health board.

This means, I suppose, someone higher up will have to decide if I'm worth the expense and time to try to save my life. Death would be my easy way out. So why do I want to survive? Why would I want to face a court in this body if Wolfgang is a child molester? To clear the family name? Ridiculous thought! That's gone down the drain a long time ago. To make excuses for my son's behavior?

No, I want him to pay for the pain he caused. Why then? Because I want to live. I need to look out for Lucas. I would love to meet my other grandson. I want to make things right. My visitor today gave me a little hope. Dear Miss Meindl might just put in a good word for me when things get really bad. Even if it is just for my wife Erna's memory's sake.

The night and the following morning are uneventful—boringly so. Not even Dr. Eichner makes an appearance. The graveyard and day nurse are both quiet, performing their routine and leaving. As per Miss Meindl's news report, the sun shone brightly. Just when I was ready to doze off again Lucas appears at my bedside. He looks all disheveled and upset as he blurts out: "She came to the school today, had me taken out of class, and started to yell at me. I ran back in, grabbed my stuff and disappeared.

"Later I saw her sitting in the Post Cafe with Eichner. One of my classmates heard them talking. Eichner is in trouble. I'm glad the hospital gave him a warning. He is not allowed to come near your room again because Miss

Meindl complained about him. Now I can come here without his interference.

"The principal did say earlier that I was old enough to choose where I want to live as long as social services finds the place appropriate. Eichner does not want to pay the monthly maintenance fee anymore. There is no way that I'm going to live with those two and their tree-hugging cult. To be dragged out of bed in the middle of the night and then sit in a dark forest chanting and praying to trees is plain idiotic. They can't make me do some stupid ancient ritual; no one else in the family wants to join them.

"Hey, did I just see you smile? Close your eyes if you agree with me. Good. The principal did say that Aunt Ingrid and Aunt Monica would take me in if I want to live with them. This is good because I like them both. You always liked them, too. They are the only nice ones in Mom's family. But they live too far away from the school and I would like to finish the final year here, near the hospital and with my friends."

At this point the nice elderly doctor comes in and introduces himself to Lucas. Dr. Wimmer explains that I have shown little improvement because of severe damage to the brain. He wants to know if there is an adult in the family he could talk to because they no longer trust Dr. Eichner and my ex-wife. Helga apparently told the hospital that she can't handle all this drama. Lucas explains to Dr. Wimmer that Doris is the only other relative on our side, but she lives in Canada and is hard of hearing.

Then Lucas turns to me and says: "Papa, how about your friend Linda? Didn't you give her power of attorney after your heart attack a few years ago? I do remember you were discussing funeral arrangements with her. Should I look through your papers and try to find her telephone number? Close your eyes if that's what you want me to do."

I have no idea who this Linda is, but I close my eyes, hoping I'm making the right decision. Lucas promises Dr. Wimmer to drop off the information the next day after school. Then he waves to me and takes off while the doctor looks at my chart and makes notes.

This was a good visit with Lucas. I can tell his anger is dissipating. Hopefully, Wolfgang did not hurt Linda's feelings like he did everyone else's. If his addiction was completely out of control, he most likely borrowed money all over the place. What am I going to do if those people appear at my hospital bed and demand payment?

Shortly after the nurse finishes with me the next morning, there is a timid knock on the door and a short, skinny woman with thin, reddish-blond hair tiptoes in. She comes up to me and looks at me carefully. Then she hangs her head and laments: "*Joa, Wolfi, des gibt joa goa net. Kenst mi go nimma*?" (*I can't believe this. Don't you recognize me?*)

She was so shocked when I showed no recognition that she voiced her disappointment in her broadest accent, a dialect that was spoken a century ago in our regional district. This was the first time I heard the true dialect. So far, all the people who spoke to me used a mix of High-German, Upper-Austrian, local Bavarian lingo, and English.

As I stare at her, I know this is a familiar face; I just can't place it. She brings her face close to mine as if trying to force me to recall her name. "Wolfgang, it's Maral. Your sister Liz and I went to school together."

As I stare at this elderly woman I can see traces of her mother Trudy in her features. The way she walks and talks reminds me of her grandmother, a narrow-minded and gossipy woman. Their place was a pigsty, literally, because they had only a small courtyard. To get to their front door you had to step over cow pads and chicken droppings and watch out for the two pigs rooting in the dirt.

They lived in a small hamlet outside our village. Most people did not mind the old lady but hated her drunken son. His neighbors swore at him when they caught him peeing out the window because he was too lazy to walk to the outhouse.

Maral makes herself comfortable on a chair and starts telling me the latest gossip about people Wolfgang knows. Apparently her brother has had health problems for years, ever since he was involved in a serious car crash. Her youngest used to be a hairdresser but has developed allergies to the chemicals in hair products.

They all go to the cemetery regularly and buy flowers for our grave, too. Next, Maral tells me how much she misses her mother, who died seven years ago. Looks like I guessed right—there are not many people left of my generation.

When the church bells ring at noon she hurriedly gets up, says goodbye, and leaves.

Lucas arrives later but without Linda's telephone number. He had too much homework and did not have enough time to look through all the drawers and boxes. What kind of squalor does he live in? Actually, I'm not too surprised. When Wolfgang and his second wife Katie resided in the duplex beside us, neither one of them did much housework. Mostly they blamed each other for their messy apartment.

At that time, Maral lived in our village. Her children played with my Canadian grandson when they came to visit and Doris was friends with her. As my health declined, Maral's mother and stepfather often came to our house to play cards with me or helped Erna around the garden.

This morning, the nurses perform their usual routines. The doctors keep away since they are still waiting for orders from higher up. I'm delighted when Maral quietly comes into the room and sits in the chair beside my bed. She seems to be genuinely upset about my—that is Wolfgang's—predicament. She tells me that his friends back home worry about him and wonder if there is anything they can do to help.

When they were kids, her brother Peppi, Wolfgang, and Fritzi, another boy who lived nearby, were nothing but trouble until our Wolfgang was sent to the seminary in Grade 5. At one point their reputation was so bad that, no matter what happened in the neighborhood, they got blamed for it.

Next, Maral starts telling me about Lotti Reuter, how she died all alone of old age. Poor Lotti. I always admired her business sense and sunny personality. Together with her mother she opened a successful store after the war. In the eighties, the big box stores opened and local businesses suffered. To make a living she added a dairy branch and did quite well selling her milk products after the local dairy operation closed.

After a while it becomes difficult to follow Maral's chatter. Too many names and places mean nothing to me. I wish I could ask her for clarification when she mentions things I think I know and would like to know more about. I can't even imagine what my old neighborhood looks like and who occupies the homes of the people I knew.

Then, out of nowhere Maral mentions Doris. They still exchange Christmas cards. Maral had hoped for a visit, but Doris needed an operation on her hand last year. It's been three years since she last saw her. While they talked over a cup of coffee Doris showed her photos of my grandson Martin and his large family. Maral laughed a bit mischievously, "Imagine at this time and age, six children! The oldest one is married already and has a little girl of his own. According to Doris, Martin calls the baby girl his little princess."

I'm relieved when the bells toll at noon and Maral says her goodbye. Now I can let my thoughts wander, let my imagination about my Canadian family run wild. There must be a way to get out of this mess, to atone for Wolfgang's sexual deprivations and then somehow get connected to the rest of my family again.

The doctors can't just let me die helplessly in this bed. They do have an obligation to tell me once the higher ups make a decision, unless they want me to suffer until the end by letting my brain deteriorate naturally from its injuries.

My sad musings are interrupted by a friendly greeting from Miss Meindl. "Good afternoon, Wolfgang. How are you doing today? I hope this Dr. Eichner has not been bothering you again. There are all sort of rumors going around, not that I believe in them, that he put a hex on Agnes and made her join a strange Celtic cult. Hard to believe, since she claims to be a devout Catholic. Her uncle is a priest, for heaven's sake."

Miss Meindl takes a deep breath, straightens her back, and pulls a newspaper from her handbag. Carefully, she unfolds the paper and, looking at me with a satisfied smile, announces: "Today is your lucky day. I found a copy of the **Sueddeutsche Zeitung**. These articles probably interest you more than the local news. Let's see. The headline says **We have at most a year to defend American democracy, perhaps less**. Timothy Snyder is a professor of history at Yale University and the author of **On Tyranny: Twenty Lessons from the Twentieth Century**. In his article, the writer compares the rise of Donald Trump with the rise of Adolf Hitler.

Oh my goodness, what's next? Well, let's see what else the professor has to say. The history of the 1930s is terribly important to Americans (and Europeans) right now, just as it is slipping from our memories.

Well, he has a point there. The young people care little about our Nazi past. They are more interested in cult idols and creatures from outer space. I'm not sure I should be reading politics to you. This is not material for a hospital patient.

Let's see. How about Facebook's Secret Rules of Deletion? The company is taking action against hate speech because it creates an intimidating and exclusionary environment. Facebook refuses to disclose the criteria that deletions are based on. Well, I hope they stop all the obscene sites, too. They are so degrading to women."

She stops, looks embarrassed, and then says quietly, "I'm sorry. I have heard you used those sites, too. It's horrible to involve young children in this filth. Horrible, just horrible."

Now she's totally flustered as she realizes that she is talking to one of those horrible people. She puts the paper down. "You have to excuse me, Wolfgang. This is a bit too nasty for me. I have to leave, get some fresh air, and, yes, I'll pray for you."

Dear Miss Meindl, she has no idea how much she confused me this afternoon. I love politics but my knowledge is almost three decades old. Who is President Trump and why is this professor comparing him to Hitler? Well, I agree that lessons are soon forgotten, but big ones, like the Second World War? How could anyone forget that? I can see why she stopped reading the article; she assumes that

Wolfgang knows who that Trump is and why he would be able to wreck democracy in the States within one year.

In the grey area I heard that the Iron Curtain came down the year I died and the Cold War ended. My goodness, things must have gone truly bad in the US since then. I wish I could tell the next person who comes in to finish reading the article. The other story about something called Facebook means even less to me. I have no idea what it is and how it could affect our minds so badly.

The term "hate speech" I understand, and that it has to be controlled, because an unruly mob gets easily carried away. Which brings us back to the 1930s and Hitler's speeches. I don't know how this Facebook is connected to sex and pornography. Playboy magazines have been around for a long time, but involving children? What is this world coming to?

This planet is in a sad state if a sweet person like Miss Meindl can't read a newspaper without being embarrassed. Poor woman. I hope walking calms her down and she finds peace in her prayers. How awfully nice of her to pray for me, too. There is no doubt that I will need all the help I can get to deal with Wolfgang's mess.

Just thinking about him makes me so angry. How could he molest children? He had a child of his own to think of. Where was Agnes when all this happened? How much did Lucas pick up from them? Knowing Dr. Eichner and his attitude toward Wolfgang, he probably heard an amplified version of the truth.

At that moment, Dr. Wimmer enters the room, looks at me, and shakes his head. "Well, Mr. Griler. I managed to get hold of your sister in Canada and this may shock you, but she said that she wants you to have the operation. She doesn't want you to die before you had a chance to suffer the consequences for your sick behavior. She needs you to face your accusers, wants you to feel their pain and their hurt. She hopes you rot in jail if you are found guilty. She struggled a bit for the right words in German but I'm sure I understood her correctly. What on earth did you do to her?"

From the door comes Lucas's voice. "My cousin is one of the people he stole from."

Then I hear Lucas's footsteps running down the hall. My insides are bursting with pent-up emotions. The machines start peeping wildly and nurses and doctors come running.

CHAPTER THREE:
Rehabilitation Woes

MY NEW QUARTERS ARE disturbing in numerous ways. The food is not bad but there is no privacy. Strict security, lack of interaction, plus disheveled, and at times delirious, fellow inhabitants in this modern judicial rehabilitation center will take time to get used to.

I'm here, waiting for my trial date.

My fellow ward mates are a colorful assortment. Illness, addiction, poverty, and homelessness have ravaged them mentally and physically. The prison hospital management does its best to keep us clean. The older patients, like myself, are mostly handicapped, either mentally or physically.

One week after my brain surgery I was released from the hospital and locked up in this institution. I had hoped for a bit of physical training to help me walk or at least regain a bit of flexibility in my hands, but the emphasis is on drug addiction treatment.

In many ways I find this amusing, since I have no desire to drink or use drugs. But how could I explain that to the people who are trying to fix an addiction that no longer exists? The doctors are already confused because I have shown no withdrawal symptoms and seem to follow instructions well, which is totally opposite from what Wolfgang's medical records for the past twenty years report.

At the beginning I was met with insults from the younger inmates, shunned by others and called names like sicko, pervert and sex maniac. The staff performed only absolutely necessary procedures and ignored me the rest of the time.

Once the pressure in my brain was reduced by the operation, my speaking abilities were back within days, though I had difficulty understanding current phrases and foreign words that had invaded the German language in the last three decades.

The police came the first week and bombarded me with questions, then got annoyed when I failed to provide answers. How could I explain that I really did not know what happened? No one would believe me if I said I wasn't Wolfgang Griler, that I'm his father.

Talking to Lucas through a protective screen was a sad and frustrating experience until we got used to the security procedures and rules. When I first managed to speak, Lucas was upset and confused that I did not know anything about our life together. Then he sort of accepted my memory lapses as a side effect of the brain damage. Often he was amused by my lack of knowledge about current events and modern equipment.

Once he realized how much I wanted to find out what was going on outside the prison walls he provided me with newspapers. A few times he brought sweets and other treats that Wolfgang used to like. One day he showed up with onion-flavored candies, which are a specialty available only in Passau. This brought back a flood of memories about my stepfather Hans, who truly believed those candies could heal sore throats and coughs.

Curiosity overcame my embarrassment as I learned about cell phones, iPads, laptops, and other modern gadgets from Lucas. One afternoon he helped me call Doris. I was so nervous that I started mumbling and Lucas had to take over the conversation. She was pleased to hear from him. They had a long talk about his schooling and my condition.

Martin's family is fine. His little granddaughter is thriving.

This morning I asked—no, begged—for a chance to go to the gym to work on my hand and leg movements. The staff did not want to wheel me to the physical rehabilitation department but gave me small dumb bells and plastic gadgets to strengthen my grip and exercise my legs. If a nurse helps me up, I can stand for a few seconds, which is a big improvement after being in a lying-down or sitting position for several months.

Doggedly, I exercise my arms and legs, from ten to fifty tries every hour or so, ignoring the laughs from my roommates: "Look at the idiot, trying to get in shape for his court appearance! Man, are you stupid! You would get more sympathy lollygagging in your wheelchair. It pays better to play dopey and helpless."

Lately I have noticed a slight change in the way people talk to me. Their attitude is slowly changing from total disgust to **maybe he is not such a horrible fellow, after all. Maybe he is sorry for what he did.**

There are several men my age in this section of the hospice who I would like to have a conversation with, but I can feel their reluctance to talk to a child molester. How I wish I could explain my weird situation in a way that a reasonable person could accept as possible.

At this point I still don't know the extent of what Wolfgang has done and how bad the consequences for his actions might be. The police only want answers to their inquiries and ignore my questions. This leaves me stagnating in a mental fog, interrupted by bursts of frightening imagined scenarios of what Wolfgang's criminal behavior could have been and what I would be accused of.

Then out of nowhere came a visit request from Maral. Surprised and confused, I pondered the question of why she would make the effort to keep in touch. She was kind to me in the hospital though she did not know that I understood what she told me. I'm amazed that she is willing to enter a prison waiting room, which is most likely a scary experience for her.

Even Miss Meindl has not come to see me since I left the hospital. Not one of Wolfgang's old friends, colleagues, or distant family members has contacted me. Out of grate-fulness for Maral's kindness and with a bit of curiosity, I give consent.

When Maral arrives a few days later she brings an Easter cake in the shape of a lamb, surrounded by brightly colored boiled eggs. The lamb-shaped cakes are a local tradition and I wonder if she had it blessed by the priest at the Easter Sunday mass. During the visit she is obviously nervous because she speaks really fast, yet so quietly that her voice is barely audible.

As I listen intently I learn that she had a pleasant Easter weekend with her daughters and grandchildren and a big dinner at her brother's house. Afterward, the whole family went to the graveyard. Maral was delighted when she saw that someone had planted pretty spring flowers on the Griler grave.

Our family always took good care of the two families plots. We often walked there in the evening to light a candle, pull weeds, or pray. Who was the mysterious gar-dener, Helga, a neighbor, one of Doris's friends? Why does Maral never mention my other grandson? She often talks about Lucas and how cute he was as a little boy.

Because of her nervousness I have great difficulty under-standing what Maral is telling me. I think I heard **sorry about this happening to you** and **they should be made accountable for what they did to you** and **how difficult it is to recover from child abuse**. This leaves me a bit confused and I have the feeling she was afraid to say out loud what was occupying her mind. Most of all, I wonder who she meant by **they?**

As I wheel myself back to my cell, the tray with the lamb cake and pretty Easter eggs on my lap, my ward mates stare and tease me. "Hey, Griler's got a treat from the Easter bunny—where is our surprise?"

Playfully, I offer them the eggs and explain how to **peck** them against each other as we did as children. The winner, whose egg survives all the hits, hoots in glee. Later, the nurse cuts the lamb, so each member of our unit gets a taste of Maral's traditional Easter cake. It tastes delicious.

Maral's mother was a good cook, too. Numerous times she secretly delivered old-fashioned Bavarian special- ties, made with lard and thick cream, to my tailor shop. My wife never developed a taste for the local deep-fried noodles and buns. She preferred fruits and vegetables. Unfortunately I had a sweet tooth and caved in to sugary temptation easily.

After supper, while my roommates are watching their favorite TV programs, my mind keeps going back to the words **they** and **child abuse**. Was she trying to tell me Wolfgang had been abused as a child? Did she mean physi- cal punishment? Was she talking about herself? I had no doubt things happened at her home that would be consid- ered unacceptable by today's standards, immoral to most people in the sixties.

Children born to families like hers often fell between the cracks. There were incidents when neighbors caught the children playing doctor and all contact with Maral and her brother was strictly forbidden. Was this what she tried to tell me? How the double standard in our small community affected her? My children or their friends could have been the instigators and she the victim. Did anyone ever try to find out the truth or were the fingers pointed automatically at the most vulnerable?

Maral's mother Trudi was a tiny but beautiful girl, full of pep and laughter. I was in the army during the time she grew into a teenager, but remember all the admiring looks she received on the way to church. Since no one in her family discouraged eager young men from chasing her, her reputation soon flew out the window. When her pregnancy started showing, rumors about the potential father followed.

The grandmother took care of the newborn baby while Trudi worked as a help in the local jewelry store. At that point the old man was more of a hindrance than help as he spent most of his time holding a beer bottle. I don't think he lived long enough to see Maral take her first steps. A few years later, a baby boy was born.

Then rumors started that Trudi met a guy through correspondence. The whole neighborhood was in an uproar when this unknown fellow moved in with her and married her within a few weeks. Not that he was a scary, dangerous man. He was a tiny, pale-looking fellow in his early thirties who had spent years in hospital.

To me it is ironic that they actually became one of the most stable, affectionate, and loving couples I know. Since they both died in the new century according to

Maral's oral report, they must have celebrated their golden wedding anniversary.

Trudi knew he had suffered terribly in WWII concentration camps, but during their first years together, she frequently gossiped that she married him for his money and did not expect him to survive a decade. Her married life turned into one big party. There were rumors and complaints about drunken affairs, loud music, and rowdy shouting. How the babies fared in all this is anyone's guess.

No matter how hard I tried, I could not find fault with the guy's polite behavior. Still, I thought I could detect a creepy, vile scent emanating from him. This left me feeling uneasy in his presence. Maybe my recent war experience had made me wary and suspicious of overwhelmingly sweet people. The man did survive a concentration camp. How could I overlook that?

His mother, an elegant, wealthy lady came to visit and lamented loudly, "I can't fathom why he would choose to dwell in this ruin of a house, why he prefers this boisterous woman to the well-mannered ladies he grew up with, and now he plans to adopt her naughty children."

By the time those children went to school, numerous changes had occurred. First, the farm animals had disappeared one by one, then construction work had started on an addition to the house. The front yard was turned into a garden with pretty flowers and vegetables.

Soon he was known as the local handyman—no job was too small or too dirty for him. He dug graves, rang the church bells and delivered food to elderly widows.

Even the most stubborn and pious members in the congregation had to acknowledge the positive changes he had brought about.

"Hey, Griler, I saw you and Maral talking in the visitors' room. I thought you like them young? Are you interested in her grandkids?"

Shocked and momentarily made speechless by this verbal attack, I stare at the drunken-looking lout who just insulted me. His broad face and lanky body seem familiar, but I can't put a name to the man.

"Man, you've really lost it, haven't you? Don't act like you can't remember me. You repeatedly came to the train station to beg me for a sniff of cocaine. The last time you ran off in a hurry when I demanded payment before handing it over. How much did you wheedle out of me, just over the last year?"

One of my biggest fears has just materialized. I'm being cornered by one of the people Wolfgang got drugs from and apparently borrowed money from. How do I deal with such a situation? Up to this point, nobody has talked to me about my financial situation. Do I get a disability pension? I can't promise this guy a payment if I haven't got a penny to spare.

Most likely, he comes from my old neighborhood since he knows Maral, but how can I ask this drug dealer who he is without looking like a total fool?

He keeps taunting me. "Yeah, now you act ignorant just like your sister. She pretended that she did not recognize me and hurriedly got onto the train to avoid further questions. What snobs you all are. Your cousin is married to my uncle; we are basically related."

No wonder I found his features familiar. He comes from that big-mouthed family one of my nieces married into. The Hartls are a huge clan, deeply rooted for many generations in a small homestead about fifty miles south of us. The men worked hard but wasted most of their free time in the pubs. Luckily, they had a knack for picking submissive, hardworking wives who looked after the kids, kept neat households, and put up with their spouses' drunken, often abusive behavior.

We were always polite with them and they tried to be friendly with us, but they were not the kind of people you invited over for coffee or had an interesting conversation with. Alcohol played a big part in our reluctance to associate with them.

This lout who is bad-mouthing me in front of my ward mates inherited the facial features of his mother, a kind but a bit pathetic woman, and the stature of his tall, lanky father, who was known for his stupid jokes and womanizing ways.

Looks like Wolfgang, while trying to find a new supplier, hooked up with him. Out of curiosity, I ask him, "How is your family doing? I lost contact with them years ago."

"Ah, that's right, you are shunning them just like your sister. This is so funny. She is still talking to you, the accused child molester, but refuses to visit us because one of our cousins played doctor with her friend's little girl forty years ago. You are such hypocrites, just like your snobby parents! My uncle was not good enough for them.

Bullshit, your cousin was lucky my uncle married her at age twenty-five, without prospects and without a dowry. Now, thanks to him, she lives in a beautiful house and enjoys the visits of her prospering children and grandkids. The last I heard, your sister lives in a tiny apartment on a measly pension. Who knows how her kid turned out? That's what pride and snobbery gets you! Just look at yourself."

Look at myself! Maybe he should look at himself, all washed out and barely functioning mental capacities. But then, how are my excellent vocabulary and inquiring mind going to help me in this damaged body? What if I never get to the point where I can establish a safe home for Lucas? How long will I end up in prison and what will I do when I get out? First of all, I need contact with the social worker who is in charge of Lucas. Then I need to find out what financial help is available to me so I can provide a bit of stability for the boy.

Our conversation seems to have exhausted Fonzi; his head droops and his eyes close. Relieved to get a break, I wheel myself as far away from him as possible, though I'm well aware of my fellow inmates staring at me. There is no chance of getting away from Wolfgang's bad deeds and reputation.

Showing my friendliest face and using my politest mode of speech, I approach the administration desk to inquire if there is an opportunity to talk to a social worker about my financial situation. The young lady at the desk gets a bit annoyed as I explain that I can't remember the names and phone numbers of the people I dealt with in the past. Finally she pulls out a file, hands it to me, pushes a pencil and a pad toward me. "Here, look through your file yourself and write down the names of people you want to contact."

The file holds a trove of information for me. This is my chance to find out as much as I can about the body I'm in and the person who occupied it before me. Writing the data down proves to be impossible as I struggle to hold the pen in my stiff fingers. Even my best attempts produce nothing but scribbles.

The young people at the table next to me start pointing at my paper and laughing at my writing attempts. Two of them come closer and make fun of my pencil markings. Their dirty minds are turning them into sexual parts and objects. Behind them an elderly man gets up, tells them to stop, and sits down across from me. "Can I help you here? What are you trying to write down?"

Reluctantly, because at this point I don't trust anyone, I explain my problem to him. "I have no memory of the last three decades. My son Lucas needs help to survive without me, in case I end up in jail for a long time."

Carefully, I read the latest information in my file and ask him to write down all the names and contact numbers that seem important. After we finish the task, he takes a look at my hands. "My sister has arthritis and she uses an attachment to hold the pen. Maybe that would work for you, too."

In the next days I obstinately practice holding a pen and try to turn my scribbles into shapes that look like letters and numbers. At one point one of the assistant aides seems to feel sorry for me and tells me to just relax and give it up. Encouraged by his interest I ask him if he heard of an attachment that would make it easier for me to hold a pen and where I would be able to find one. Shaking his head at me, he walks away but promises to talk to a trainer at the rehab department.

Thinking about being able to write again gives me hope. Instead of wasting my time pondering this dreary situation I could document previous experiences and explain my current circumstances to Doris and her family. Old poems, political rants, and jingles I wrote throughout my life flash through my mind. How I would love to find a copy of the book of my poems Wolfgang and his first wife printed for my 65th sixty-fifth birthday. What happened to my journal—did it end up in the trash? Does Doris have the little book of poems and letters I sent to her the year before I passed away?

When Lucas comes to visit I show him my list of names and phone numbers and ask him if he knows any of those people. Unfortunately he only remembers the name of his current social worker, but he is willing to ask her which government department would be responsible in a case like mine. He will also try to find out how I can get an appointment with a legal and financial adviser.

The boy seems to be glad to see me thinking about our future, but sounds a bit surprised by my new interests.

Obviously, Wolfgang did not plan ahead, maybe did not even manage to provide bare necessities for the boy. After Lucas leaves, I thumb through the Spiegel magazine he has brought for me, just in case there is an article more interesting than the report on the G-7 leaders' summit.

The heading **Donald Trump's Triumph of Stupidity** catches my eye and, though I love political commentaries, I experience a moment of dread. Anything written about the new US president seems to have that effect on me, a kind of DE-ja-vu, bringing back memories of the years before WWII, the tension, the instability, the lies and the fears. The threat that the US might pull out of the Paris Agreement will have very real consequences all over the world.

Like Merkl said, **If the world's largest economic power pulls out, the field will be left to the Chinese**. They could take advantage of this opportunity. This is not only about saving the earth; conserving energy is also good for the economy.

Trump is clearly suffering from an overblown ego and fears smart people. His mantra is **Make America great again**. Does he think being the US president is a game show, where he can make up the rules and then yell **You are fired** at anyone who opposes him or merely disagrees with him?

My Spiegel moment is interrupted by a young man I have not seen before. "Hey, Wolfgang, good to see you ended up here, too. What did you do? Did you try to rip off my silly old grandma? She wouldn't let me stay in the house with her but she rented out the top floor to you and your kid. Strange old biddy! What happened to the kid?"

Before I have a chance to respond, one of the guards calls out the name **Walters**. The young man reluctantly walks over to the reception desk. I'm grateful for being spared an uncomfortable confrontation with someone who obviously knows me and may have had an unpleasant transaction with me. While talking to the social worker he keeps turning around and staring at me. Maybe Lucas can tell me who this Walters is.

The next morning it is my turn to be called to the reception desk. The grumpy clerk informs me that a legal aid counselor named Stilz is asking to see me. My immediate thought is: oh no, something happened to Lucas, but Mrs. Stilz explains that she is here to provide legal counsel. First, she wants me to tell her my side of the story.

The moment I say that I have a memory loss and can't recall anything that happened before the suicide attempt, she looks at me suspiciously. Then she explains that there is not much she can do to help me unless I give her permission to review my medical and police reports. I make a serious attempt to scribble Wolfgang Griler on the appropriate consent forms. As she packs up her papers I ask her if she could tell me who will be paying her fees and if she has any idea what my financial situation is. She promises to find out and let me know what happens next.

After lunch, George, the nice assistant aide, beckons me to join him at a table in a quiet corner. There is another fellow sitting there who seems to be assessing me with a stern but inquiring look. Once I maneuvered my wheelchair into the small space at the table, he explains that he is from the physical rehabilitation department and came over to check out my hand and finger movements.

He grabs my hands, twists them into various positions, and inspects each finger separately before turning to me. "If it weren't for that fellow's insistence, I would not have come. As far as I can see, there is some strength in your left hand and your thumb is movable. The fingers on your right hand are too stiff; I doubt you will ever be able to get much use out of them. Here is an exercise ball to work on your grip. One of the best things for you would be a keyboard. Since it is not likely that you will get a piano in here, you could try a computer and learn to type with your left hand."

Why did I not think of this myself? Of course that is the perfect solution! All those hours I spent on my beloved typewriter, clicking away on my poems and articles. When I ask Lucas if he could find me a typewriter, he looks at me in disbelief and then starts laughing hysterically. "Get real, where would I get hold of a typewriter? A garbage dump or a museum? They no longer exist—everyone is using computers."

Embarrassed, I inquire how much a simple, older computer would cost. My explanation that I would use it only for typing stories confuses him. "What kind of stories would you write and how would you print them? Don't you remember, they have banned you from using the Internet because you were downloading child porn sites and got caught? You would have to ask a guard how to get permission to access a rehabilitation department computer or if you can bring one in from the outside."

When I ask Lucas if he knows a young man named Walters, he wants to know why. I tell him that this Walters came here yesterday and started ranting about his grandma and me.

According to Lucas we were able to rent the top floor of a house in the middle of town thanks to Karl, a former co-worker, who was the landlady's son and the angry young man's uncle. I also found out that my—that is, Wolfgang's—drug problem was no secret. He had been hospitalized several times and had been on Methadone for years.

A few days later I am told to go to the visitors' reception area because a Mrs. Walters demands to see me. Surprised and a bit panicked, I wheel myself down the hall, all the while attempting to overcome my fears that Lucas might be in trouble. The frail, ancient-looking, but totally charming lady eases my worries right away. Her greeting is heartfelt and her voice is kind and gentle: "Good day, Wolfgang. I heard from Karl that Toni saw you in here. You must excuse this delayed visit but, as you know, I was in the hospital with a broken hip at the time you decided to jump off the Penny Bridge.

"In hindsight I keep reprimanding myself for not acting when I recognized the symptoms of severe depression in you. I should have talked you into getting treatment. I kept telling myself that you would come out of it just fine. I went through a similar situation with my son Peter, Toni's father. Later, I regretted not being there when he needed me most. That's why I practice tough love with Toni and don't let him get away with thievery and lies. At least he is still alive, but what a waste of life as a homeless addict, in and out of rehab and jail."

My mind is reeling, trying to make sense of all this information. Wolfgang was fortunate to have such a sweet and caring landlady. Did not having her around after her accident affect his mental condition? She was blaming an icy patch on the sidewalk for her fall. Did he feel responsible in some way? From our conversation I can tell that dear Mrs. Walters does not fault him. She actually seemed to enjoy Wolfgang's company and says she misses their interesting discussions.

Hearing a positive report on Wolfgang does not lessen my dread of the future but gives me a bit of hope that I will not have to face the coming trials all by myself. There are people who care in spite of the sexual deprivations I am— he is—accused of. How much will it take for Lucas, Mrs. Walters, Maral, and volunteers like Miss. Meindl to stop being kind and helpful? Will Doris ever be able to look at me without disgust?

All this talk about molestation and sexual abuse is confusing to me. Seems to me that behavior like unwanted touching, verbal garbage, whistling, and embarrassing stares by obnoxious, lewd men we used to laugh at, is now pursued in court as sexual harassment. I'm all in favor of stopping sexual harassment, but is a courtroom the proper place if we can't provide solid evidence?

The effect of molestation on small children is especially sad. There has to be punishment for the abuser without harming the child even more. How can lawyers rely on a young, imaginative child's vague story and determine what is fact and what is imagination? Do you choose to err on the side of the helpless victim? Will a wealthy community patriarch get away with sexual crimes because he can afford the best lawyer? Is a child from a derelict area less deserving of justice than a spoiled, rich brat?

"Wolfgang, you seem to be an intelligent man, what made you give in to deviant sexual urges without thought for consequences? Was this a game to see how much you could get away with? Maybe you didn't give a damn, lived for a fleeting moment of sexual titillation? Did you see sexual acts as a payback for being hurt yourself as a youngster? Are you suffering from an inferiority complex? Does overpowering another human being give your ego a temporary lift?"

Mrs. Walters pauses and looks me straight in the eye. "I know that you think of yourself as a caring father and I know that Lucas loves you, so how can you reconcile this relationship you have with your son to the fact that you are a child abuser?"

To hear the thoughts that have been occupying my mind ever since I ended up in this body voiced in such an intelligent way is mesmerizing. The way she looked at me—hurt, disappointed, confused—made me want to comfort her. I was close to telling her that I would never have considered giving in to such urges.

What was the point, though, she would never believe me if I said that I was not Wolfgang. For Lucas's sake, I have to find a solution and atone for the past. Atonement is the only way for me to go forward.

"Mrs. Walters, can you help me find a way to help the victims? How can I atone for the damage that was done to them, ease their pain?"

She looks at me thoughtfully and shakes her head. "Atone? Impossible! The way the legal system is set up there is no room for atonement, only for punishment. Hopefully, there is enough good evidence at the trial to convict you so your victims can see justice being served. A guilty verdict and maximum jail time for you will help those poor youngsters put their anger, hurt, and frustrations behind them. Then their wounds can slowly heal as they grow up. At least this would give them a chance to restructure their lives."

CHAPTER FOUR:
Unique Presentations

AROUND THE MIDDLE OF June, Lucas arrived, grinning all over his face. "Papa, I found a special gift for you, you will never guess what it is. On Monday, I ran into Miss Meindl at the train station and, while we talked about you, I mentioned that you wanted a typewriter. She laughed and then told me she had the perfect specimen for you in the attic. Her brother dropped it off last night. Here comes the guard with the carrying case. He just inspected it. What do you say—ready to take a look at it?"

The guard pops the case open and places the typewriter on my lap. It's a portable model, just like the one I used to have. I'm delighted. Picking up a piece of paper from the stack at the bottom of the case takes me a few tries; putting it through the roller and adjusting it takes even longer. I type THANK YOU, LUCAS and proudly hold it up for him to see. He is so excited that he is jumping up and down like

a little kid. Before he leaves, he tells me that Miss Meindl
will drop in next time she is in town. She has a sick sister
who needs her help most days.

Thanks to the exercise ball, the fingers on my left hand
are more flexible than when the trainer checked them out,
but there is little progress with my right hand. Writing
with the left hand is quite a struggle, but, slowly, my letters
become readable. Learning to type is a bit of a challenge,
too, though not half as difficult as practicing my handwriting. Every free moment I type, and slowly, with one finger,
word after word, line by line, I put down my thoughts.

As I read my emerging prose, I have the feeling that I'm
in a time warp. Visions of family members, the tailor shop,
and the old neighborhood flood my mind. An intense
session on the typewriter helps me forget that I'm stuck in
Wolfgang's body and that the preliminary trial is coming
up in August.

Standing on my own two feet to hear the court's decision
is slowly becoming a reality. At this point I can walk about
two meters on crutches without losing my balance. A great
deal of my time is still wasted on drug addiction counseling and support groups but, last week, for the first time,
I was allowed to go to the physical rehabilitation center.
The trainer, who did not exactly welcome me, taught me
how to use a machine that might be helpful with regaining
strength in my legs.

Quite like the helplessness I experienced in the final
years of living with multiple sclerosis, there are many
bodily functions that I can't handle by myself. I'm trying

to reach a point where I no longer need an aide to get me ready in the morning and at night before bed. Brushing my teeth with the left hand was a major achievement.

These last few weeks I rarely saw Lucas, as he is busy studying for his final exams. Hopefully, he will pass with good grades and get into a college. From what he told me, the choice is no longer what you want to be, but what opportunities are available to you. In the sixties when my kids graduated, there was a frenzy to hire young people because so many new companies were springing up. Trades like mine, on the other hand, were no longer viable since mass-produced suits and coats were much cheaper.

My only visitors were Misses Meindl and Maral. "This rehabilitation center is much too intimidating. I was scared to come by myself. Then I met Miss Meindl at the bakery and we decided to visit you together. How are you holding up? I brought you Bavarian dumplings, still fresh from lunch today. Miss Meindl has paper for your typewriter. Are you really starting to type, just like your father? Do you remember how you used to make fun of his poems and stories?"

Miss Meindl shakes her head. "As we age we get to be more like our parents, just look at yourself, Maral. You have perfected your mother's speech pattern and you walk like her, too. Wolfgang, years ago, your mother gave me a copy of your father's book and I must say I found some of his poems quiet charming and amusing. There was a lot of talent, but too often he got lost in emotional outbursts and political rants. You know, writing might help you work through your issues, could even help you fight against your sexual perversions. What kind of stories or poems are you working on?"

A bit embarrassed, I explain that typing with one finger of my left hand is a slow process and at this point I'm not sure where my writing is going to take me. Then it occurs to me that Miss Meindl might still be in possession of my little book. I get so excited that I barely manage to say the words: "Do you still have the book of poems, Erna, em… my mother, gave you?"

"Of course, I'll bring it to you on my next visit, though that might be a while. Poor Lena is not recovering well from her chemo and needs my help on a daily basis."

Maral had been quiet but now she suddenly speaks up. "Wolfgang, if you want your father's writing, our Peppi found a large envelope filled with papers and photos when he helped the guy who bought your house clean out the shed. He might have kept them. If you would like those papers, I can ask him to mail them to you. I know that you don't want to see him; he tried that once and you just yelled at him to get lost."

The visit from Mrs. Stiltz, the legal counselor, was a big letdown. My financial situation is in a terrible state: unpaid bills, bad debts, important forms were not completed and help from social workers was either ignored or downright refused. Looks like Wolfgang was unable to live within his budget, either because he did not care to or because he was not mentally fit to accomplish the required tasks.

At least the counselor promised to get me copies from the police files. In a few days I will know the severity of the crimes I'm accused of. Reading those documents will be a nightmare. Knowing that a whole courtroom of people will be looking at me during the trial will be demoralizing. No wonder Wolfgang tried to take the fast way out, and now I have to face the awful mess he left behind. I'm beginning to despise him to the point where I want to beat the shit out of him. Then I feel ashamed and wonder where his spirit ended up. Is there a separate hell for sex offenders?

Today is solstice. Our village used to light a bonfire. The mayor held a speech, young people performed traditional dances, and the volunteer firemen built a human pyramid. I usually ended up in the bottom row because I was tall and strong. As newlyweds, Erna and I joined the other young couples leaping over the fire.

This morning I was called to the reception desk and told a Mr. Velji wanted to talk to me. I wondered who this surprise visitor could be. The middle-aged man standing in the visitors' room looked southern European, maybe even Arabic. He introduced himself as Ahmed's father. There were a few minutes of silence as both of us tried to form our thoughts into words. We were total strangers, after all.

Next, Mr. Velji told me in broken German, mixed with English words, that Mrs. Walters offered the apartment I had occupied to him and his family. He asked if I had any objections if his family used my furniture, because up to now they had been housed in refugee quarters. There were also numerous boxes to be sorted and moved. Would I be able to make a list of what I wanted to keep and what could be given away or recycled

This was a bit of a dilemma since I had no idea what Wolfgang kept in those boxes. I explained to Mr. Velji about my memory loss and that I could not recall what was left in the storage area. Lucas could decide which items he wanted to save and the rest could be given away. If there were books, I might want to keep a few of the classics and I would need personal items like documents, photos, clothes, shoes, and toiletries. From Mr. Velji's smile, I gathered that he was pleased with the outcome from our conversation. After some small talk, we shook hands and said a friendly goodbye.

Today I found out from Mrs. Stiltz that I won't be able to read the police reports. I will have to see a doctor instead. He will assess my mental capabilities and prepare a report about my sexual tendencies and estimate the odds of turning me from a sexual pervert into a normal man.

This is going to be such a confusing counseling session, worse than the drug and alcohol addiction rehabilitation program. How can I possibly participate in this sexual per-version assessment without looking like a total idiot? I will be expected to feel shameful, contrite, and remorseful, but all I can feel is anger, often hate, toward Wolfgang.

My own sexual experiences were limited, a bit like what I have heard described as vanilla sex. Even the idea of dis-cussing sexual acts with a doctor is embarrassing to me. I'm sure that, whatever Wolfgang's perversions were, they would be contrary to what I believed in and clearly contradict the morals I tried to teach him.

Since I could not convince the medical profession that I had no desire to abuse drugs or alcohol, how could I make them believe me if I said I had no urges to molest or rape anyone? Violence goes against my nature, I would never, ever physically hurt or sexually abuse a child or a woman.

The psychologist Dr. Kohlberger turned out to be a jolly, short, middle-aged man. He was a lot less jolly after our session because my honest answers totally confused and annoyed him. No matter what I said did not fit the profile of a sex offender. My answers made me look like a total liar. At one point I was ready to make up a reply that might come out of a pervert's mouth, but stopped myself in time when I thought what such a move might lead to.

The whole hour was a waste of time for both of us: he did not get one useful answer to his standard questions and I could not help him, because I was not the person he thought I was. Dr. Kohlberger left with the warning. "Mr. Griler, this is no time for silly games. Until I get your full cooperation and honest participation, I cannot file the required report and this foolishness will count against you in court."

After he left, I rolled a new sheet of paper in the typewriter. Then I attempted to put down my thoughts about the session with Dr. Kohlberger. Carefully, I replayed his questions and tried to think of answers that would not challenge the psychologist's professional skills, but would provide me with clues as to Wolfgang's criminal acts.

Would he agree to let me take a polygraph test to prove my innocence?

Up to this point I have heard bits and pieces, mostly in the form of indirect suggestions and expressions of disgust and hate. The details are missing or blurred, but since I'm seen as the molester, nobody tells me anything. I am expected to know the crimes committed by the body I'm occupying. Queries from me give the impression that I'm trying to deny or justify the acts. Not admitting to sexual depravity basically means I'm calling the victims liars.

Hopelessly I stare at the blank page. Even Mrs. Walters believes there is no chance of avoiding a trial. Still the word *atonement* lingers in my head. Atonement for one's sins was a huge part of my Catholic upbringing, though in most cases it only meant praying a certain number of the Lord's Prayer or Holy Mary's, according to the priest's instructions. Like most people, I believe that criminals should pay for their sins, as simple as: you stole it, replace it; you robbed him, give him back the money and add extra to make up for the trauma.

This method would not work with a sexual pervert, since you can't take back the damage and you can't repair it, either. Would a child even want to face the molester and hear an apology? Tribal societies handed out their own judgments in the form of physical punishment, even torture. In Arabic countries, stoning, chopping off fingers/ hands, or whipping are part of the punishment, often performed by neighbors and angry mobs without legal interference. Other societies have prison work camps, similar to the Russian gulags in Siberia.

What is a reasonable time to lock up a pervert, who has harmed one, a dozen, maybe hundreds of children?

"Hey, Griler, I see you've got a typewriter. Ever heard of a computer? Man, you suck! Are you writing an article for a pornographic magazine? A child molestation poem?"

Annoyed, I look up at Walters, who so rudely interrupted my thoughts. He actually seems much calmer today. Even his voice sounds more cynical than angry. In the spur of the moment, I decide to play his game. "Kid, what do you know about sex, living on the street, dirty, smelly, and unkempt? Do you have any idea what damage you do while drunk or stoned out of your mind? You may have behaved worse than Wolfgang did, and just don't know about it. How can you be so sure no one could point a finger at you and accuse you of sexual harassment or even rape?"

Looks like I hit a nerve because he turns his head, walks away, and then yells over his shoulder: "Shut up, you stupid pervert. You crippled idiot! Girls always liked me, they were chasing me, I never had to force myself on anyone."

This certainly was a bad move on my part. Now all the guys within hearing distance are staring at me and making nasty comments. At my age, I should know better than to challenge an angry young man and the buddies he made during previous rehabilitation and jail stays. Luckily, a guard steps in and things quiet down immediately. Hopefully, this will be the end of this episode.

How wrong I was. The incident was the beginning of new nightmares. Odd things started to happen. My pillow disappeared. The typewriter paper was ripped in half. Someone wrote "pervert" in red ink above my headboard. Then odd items were thrown at me in the hallway—half-eaten buns, wet facecloths, apple cores, even a tennis ball. Mostly they hit the wheelchair but any solid objects landing on my head hurt.

No matter how hard I tried to catch the culprit, I never did. There were too many doors leading into the main hallway. Then the harassment during meal time started, foul language aimed at me, punctuated with leftover food. Security must have seen all this on their cameras and decided to let it go.

When I asked if I could have my meals in the cell, the guard, who looked a lot like the louts who harassed me, laughed. "Griler, you are an idiot. Nobody gets room service. Especially not you."

Then one day the guy who had helped me by writing down the telephone numbers from my folder sat down on my table. "You know, Griler, you are a strange bird. You, a sex offender act like a monk and preaching to addicts. Did you try listening to Toni? You have to have some idea how homeless kids get treated by the perverts looking for a victim. To those young lads, you are one of the evil guys who degraded them, abused them, and at times nearly killed them. Each one of those men knew just how desperate the boy was for a fix. Think about that next time, before you get the urge to talk down to those youngsters with crazy sermons. They are the victims, for heaven's sake. You are the evil predator."

"I'm sorry, that thought never occurred to me. Do you think Toni really might want to talk to me?"

He stared at me. "Why not, what have you got to lose? By the way, my name is Otto Morstein. I think your brother was a grade below me at the seminary. Nice guy, good soccer player. Hey, wait, weren't you one of the boys who shut themselves up in the bell tower and rang the bells whenever you felt like it? Stayed in that dark tower all night, kept sitting on the trap door, no matter how hard the adults yelled as they tried to lift it? How old were you crazy kids? Eleven? Twelve? That took guts. Boy, were the teachers and the monks mad."

Of course I remembered that scandalous event. Erna freaked out when the principal from the seminary called and demanded we come there as fast as possible and get Wolfgang out of the bell tower. Those little idiots were making demands like better food, less homework, etc. We were afraid he would get thrown out of that private school. They gained nothing but punishment. Wolfgang lost his weekends with the family and had to wash school windows with his fellow culprits instead.

While I was lost in my thoughts, Otto vanished from the table. Luckily, the rowdies have settled down and lost interest in me. Quietly, I wheel myself away. In my cell, I sit beside the bed and stare at the typewriter. Where did the excitement about being able to write again go? Well, if I end up in jail for a few years, I will have plenty of time to type my life story. I need to focus on the present, figure out how I can prove that I'm not Wolfgang, or—more likely—accept punishment for his sexual crimes and make the best of the situation.

Help arrives from unexpected quarters when I'm handed a huge envelope. Eagerly, I rip open the flap and in the process spill the contents all over my bed. I sort them into stacks of photos, documents, letters, and—what totally puzzles me—a huge pile of thin, long strips of papers with writing on them. Among the photos, I'm delighted to recognize the beloved faces of my children at different stages in their lives. Chubby little Doris in a white confirmation dress is holding a fancy candle almost as tall as she was at age nine. Handsome Hubert is posing in his soccer uniform. Lizzerl is sleeping in the baby carriage and a preschool Wolfgang laughs at the camera.

What happened to his beautiful smile, his easy-going personality? Picking out photos of him, I sort them by age, then slowly work my way through the stack. There is no denying that the expression on his face gets angrier year by year, turns grim as he becomes an adult.

As his father, I knew he was often unhappy, but hoped he would work out his problems. Most worrisome is the dis-connectedness showing up on his face about a decade after my death. His body was there with his family, his mind was clearly elsewhere. Except when he looked directly at Lucas—then he smiled adoringly.

An object hitting the back of my head stops my musings. Liquid is running down my neck and I can smell over-ripe tomato. Laughter erupts in the hallway until the running footsteps fade away. With my stiff fingers it takes me forever to wipe myself clean. Then I try to rub the splashes off my wheelchair and the bedspread. Even the photos and papers have tiny red spots all over them.

Without my physical limitations, I would probably be able to laugh it off as a silly prank. Now the extra work and frustrations brought on by a rotten tomato make me cry.

Come on, Joseph, what happened to the old prankster? Where is your sense of humor?

Next thing, Toni is standing beside me with paper towels and helps me clean up. "Hey, Griler, man, you are clumsy. Let me finish this off."

His kindness takes me by surprise and I watch in disbelief as he polishes my wheelchair. Then he tells me to wait and disappears out the door. Within minutes, he is back with three shoe boxes. He puts a pile of the documents and photos in each one. When he comes to the paper strips, he lifts one up, reads it, and looks at me, confused. "What the hell is that, a new format of writing poems?"

Now I'm curious and read one, too. **What sex between ducks explains about humans.** Since I said it out loud, he starts laughing hysterically and I get caught up in his hilarity. For the first time since I got stuck in this body, I burst out in laughter and it feels darn good. Toni picks up another long strip. New Facebook rules saying **fucking Muslims** is not allowed; calling them **fucking migrants** is. He shakes his head and, before I can thank him for his help, he walks out the door.

The interval with Toni left me in a happy mood, but it also took me off my guard. I was totally unprepared when two big guys grabbed my wheelchair in the hall and a third punched me repeatedly in the face. They rocked me back and forth, harder and faster each time, with my body helplessly bouncing from side to side. Then they counted to three and tipped the chair over, dumping me on the floor. There was loud laughter, I felt cold water on my lap and hot liquid splashing on my back. Suddenly, the alarm went off and my attackers disappeared. I kept my eyes shut tightly to stop the tears from running down my face.

In emergency, they cleaned up my face, checked it for damage, patched me up, took X-rays of my right arm and then put it in a cast. The whole experience was frightening and put me back a notch in my recovery efforts. My back is still sore from the burning hot coffee and my broken arm is throbbing, but otherwise I'm managing all right.

Toni was my first visitor and he made it quite clear: he and his friends had nothing to do with the louts who hurt me. The rumor is that Fonzi is responsible. This could be weird. Am I facing a full-fledged war between the Hartl and Griler clans? How the hell am I going to fight back in this condition? Worse, I can't even afford to buy myself a chocolate bar. Where would I find the cash to pay anyone for protection?

While Toni was here this morning, he helped me look through the box filled with the papers—mostly unpaid bills, a few letters from people I did not know, a postcard from a Sister Magdalena (I recognized the handwriting as

Katie's because we used to write each other long letters of complaints), and—surprise, surprise—several cards from Doris. Looks like she was sending Lucas pocket money until about a year ago.

At least I found her address. Toni prepares an envelope for me and finds an international stamp. All I have to do is write a few sentences. Dear Doris… with love, your Papa, no… brother, no… Wolfgang! How on earth can I make this work without making her more angry?

Maybe I begin with an apology, but how do I phrase it without knowing what I have to be sorry and ashamed for? Of course I can start by asking her about her family, begging for a photo, maybe. Then there is Lucas, with his graduation in a few weeks. I wonder if I should mention my upcoming trial date.

Well, click after click, with many stops in between, I manage a page and a half, mostly because I got carried away after I read the newest article about the US president. Half of my letter turned into a political rant.

My signature looks terribly clumsy, bringing to mind a child's first attempt at writing in long-hand. I keep staring at the letter and feel like a cheater, like someone who has hastily copied a fellow pupil's homework.

Another session with Dr. Kohlberger, not much different from the last one. In spite of my plans to be accommodating and not to upset the good doctor, he storms out of the meeting room. All I did was ask one question. "Into which category would you put Wolfgang's sexual deprivations," because he had explained the different categories into which sexual crimes fall according to the law.

In hindsight I can see that my question sounds callous, but I had no intention of insulting him. Do you know anyone who would not want to know what they are accused of? I had the feeling that he was ticked off by my asking the question in the third-person form. This, he probably believes, means I do not want to take responsibility for my actions. He has a good point there, but I am not Wolfgang, I did not commit those crimes and I will not simply give in to his prodding.

Actually, I'm feeling proud of myself. Joseph is no longer sitting on the fence. He is standing up for what he believes. Wouldn't Max get a kick out of this turn of events? After I got beaten up, I was in a terrible state of mind. All I could think of was how to get out of this stupid body and escape back into the grey fog, hopefully meet up with Max, and forget about earth, Wolfgang, even Doris and her family.

Lately, Toni, the young drug addict, drops in and lightens my mood. Who would have expected a friendship to grow between two such unlikely characters? Yesterday, he arrived waving a book in my face. "Griler, you know, every psychologist should be made to read this. Jailing addicts is all wrong. Treating our habit as an illness would stop small crimes and cut off the cash flow to criminal empires. Only mobsters benefit from our misery."

According to the book, the war on drugs in America was set off in 1904, when a teenager heard his neighbor scream in agony, caused by her withdrawal symptoms from laudanum, a mix of opium and alcohol. This experience apparently influenced this young man's life. He became prohibition agent Anslinger.

In the mid-twenties, at the height of prohibition, he was promoted from a prohibition agent in the Bahamas to running a Washington, DC, federal prohibition department. From the war on booze he graduated to attacks on narcotics. At first, there was not much political interest, but he kept pushing his biased theories anyway. Who would oppose or challenge him, when he was married to the daughter of the US treasury secretary?

Toni got a big kick out of the chapter dealing with marijuana. He read aloud to me: "This happens when you smoke weed. First, you fall into a delirious rage. Then you will be gripped by dreams of an erotic character. Then you will lose the power of connected thought. Finally, you will reach the inevitable end point, insanity."

In the eighties, twenty-nine scientific experts out of thirty were saying it would be wrong to ban marijuana and that the side effects were widely misrepresented in the press. Still, Anslinger kept pushing his agenda that marijuana could turn men into wild beasts.

My own perception of smoking pot was not that much different, I fully believed that getting stoned would seriously damage Wolfgang's brain. He started at a young age, barely sixteen years old. We had serious fights about his drug use, daily screaming matches. At times I got so frustrated that I hit him.

After Toni left I picked up the book. It was called **Chasing the Scream** and I quickly leafed through it. Though I agree with the strategy of drug busts and jailing dealers, I do believe that addicts need rehabilitation and support to get over their drug dependency.

As Toni said, "I did not declare one day: today is the day I'm becoming an addict. In the beginning, drinking and using were just dares, challenges between friends. At one point I realized I was hooked. I basically medicate myself with alcohol and street drugs to overshadow my insecurities and forget bad memories from my childhood."

The beginning chapters provide samples of how far addiction goes back, at times covering several generations. What shocked me were the statistics showing that the majority of pot smokers and cocaine users live in the Upper West Side of New York, not in the Bronx, or Brownsville section. In the expensive neighborhoods, people supposedly use as much as in the poor ones, but the effect on their lives is dramatically different. The wealthy addicts get sent to rehabilitation centers and the poor ones to jail.

Today, Toni brought a local newspaper to show me two articles. Washington State legalized marijuana, but they are now worried Trump might put a stop to it. According to this paper, Canada is allowing medical use with prescriptions and this year appointed a committee to investigate how to regulate the growing and distribution of pot on a country-wide basis.

Even though we became friends, I'm still afraid to ask Toni the questions I have been struggling with for a while.

He talks about childhood trauma and depression and is impressed by the new rehabilitation methods in Portugal. Then why does he get upset with Mrs. Walters and his Uncle Karl when they offer him counseling, schooling, training, shelter, whatever else might be required, to keep him away from the streets and drugs? How come Toni refuses their help? What is stopping him from changing his lifestyle? The way he talks, he has never taken rehabilitation seriously. Will nothing tempt him to really make an effort, give it 100 percent?

When he gets carried away in a diatribe about his childhood, his father's addiction, and the pain and hurt caused by it, he sounds like a scratched record. You can have an interesting conversation with him up to a certain point, and then his clear, smart voice seems to cut out. Something is blocking the connection from having intelligent thoughts to actually making the decision to put them in action. He keeps repeating the same cycle of positive thinking and then losing control.

What if Lucas falls into the same trap? Wolfgang was on drugs—surely Lucas was aware of his condition. How often did he get neglected, maybe even abused, when Wolfgang was high and insensible to his surroundings? The effect on Lucas must have been wide reaching. No good parent would have let his kids associate with Lucas, never mind go to his home. Teachers might not have understood his complicated family situation or might give up on Lucas without giving him a chance.

From what I have seen, Lucas is a great kid, but what if he just hides his pain and insecurities, and they come to the surface later in life? There is no family from our side to guide him, care for him, support him, if needed. I have no idea how much help he would receive from his mother's side. He did talk about two aunts he liked. Would they be there for him if he needed them?

Lucas should be getting his report card this week. He is pretty nervous about it. I hope he passes and gets to graduate. That will be one positive thing in his life, a big step forward. The trial will bring nothing but dread and misery into my life; I don't want him to be around at that time. Maybe he can get a summer job near one of his aunts. Being far away from the courthouse would be best for him while the shady parts of Wolfgang's life get dragged to the surface.

CHAPTER FIVE:
Fears and Nightmares

WHAT A TERRIBLE NIGHT, being chased by weird monsters with human features I was not able to recognize. Dream after dream, I saw glimpses of people I once knew, popping in and out of my sight, confusing and frightening me. My head is still spinning from this strange assortment of faces teasing and deriding me. They resembled relatives, friends, acquaintances, and people I met in different stages of my existence, mixed with hateful neighbors, Nazi-thugs, and all those who put me down, disrespected me, and ignored me my whole life. Even Max made an appearance through a violet smoke-spewing tunnel to yell at me. "Focus, Joseph, focus."

I believe Dr. Kohlberger is partly responsible for my nightmares with his constant derogatory remarks about my mental state. Deep down, I have the feeling he would like to write me off as insane, but he can't come up with an appropriate label for the strange, supposedly mental degeneration or insanity he thinks I suffer from. The current fad with bipolar or attention-deficit-disorder diagnosis will not work in my case, would not convince a judge or jury that I did not understand the seriousness of the sex crimes.

On top of this, I recently read an article in the *Sueddeutsche Zeitung* about an artist's schizophrenia. The description of his illness touched deep-seated fears and disturbed me greatly. During the final years of my own life, I experienced strange episodes where words came out of my mouth that I knew were horrible. Yet I seemed to have lost control—not only over my thoughts, also over what I actually said.

In his panic moments, the artist believes things that he knows are not possible or true in his normal state. Does accusing a neighbor of having an affair with my wife fall in the same category? Once I actually put this craziness in a note and posted it on the local church's public announcement board. Of course, in my sane moments, I was well aware that this was fiction created by a jealous mind. Erna would not even have considered kissing that particular man, would never, ever have consented to an affair with him.

Could that also have happened to Wolfgang? Did his brain make up a reality with no connection to his actual surroundings? Was his perceived reality a safe haven from his guilt feelings, a haven that blocked out childhood horrors or a hide-out to escape his own deprived sexual urges and acts? There were times when he was unapproachable, sitting cross-legged in a corner of the attic or smoking pot in the shed at the end of our yard. His strange moods certainly played a big role in the failure of his marriages and the resulting divorces. From what Max told me, Wolfgang never cared enough about anything to make an effort. At the slightest hint of trouble, he simply disappeared, discussion over, case closed.

The artist in the article wrote secret messages to himself—mostly warnings, advice, and at times just crazy stuff, unintelligible nonsense that no one was able to unscramble. The big question is: when can a patient be forced to accept treatment and/or be committed? Walking barefoot in the park in freezing temperatures is not enough! Life-threatening self-harm and attacks on family or innocent bystanders definitely are!

Why does Dr. Kohlberger think I—that is Wolfgang—should be in a mental institution, not a jail? What is the reason for his desire to avoid a trial? Does he want to save the children from testifying and avoid court costs or is it because, once Wolfgang is declared insane, he can have him locked up indefinitely, not just for a few years?

Is there someone behind the scene, pushing for a diagnosis? Could there be another sexual predator involved who needs to silence Wolfgang, someone with the power to pull strings and get results? Or are these questions simply a sign that my old distrust of doctors is messing with my mind, making me paranoid?

Luckily, my fellow inmates have left me alone lately. Even the Hartl relative by marriage, Fonzi, has not said a word to me since I was beaten up. Once in a while, Otto gives me a friendly nod when he walks past my table. Toni has been quiet, too. His sentence is almost over and he is worried about how he will handle life on the outside.

Karl and Mrs. Walters have visited him a few times and usually stop to exchange a few words with me. They both told me that Lucas is fitting in well with the Velji family; he and Ahmed are worried about their test results, anxious to get graduation over with.

My typing is sporadic but a bit faster now. I have not managed anything beside lists of things to do and notes to myself. Once a week, I draft a letter for Doris, to keep her up to date with a little gossip and a bit of political ranting. So far, I have not gotten a reply from her. Even Miss Meindl and Maral seem to have forgotten me.

Mrs. Stiltz came the other day with bankruptcy documents to fill out, an urgent task because court proceedings are starting next month. Once my debts are settled, I will be able to save a few pennies here and there and can give Lucas a little financial help when needed.

Day after day, I attempt to convince myself that I enjoy my current quiet time, but with each day, the heaviness I noticed when I came out of my coma seems to increase a bit. My body feels like a scale to which a small weight is added each time I fall asleep.

Reading about Trump makes me worry about Lucas's future. The article of his denials regarding his Russian connection is hard to swallow. They have all been his buddies in shady global deals to gain wealth and power. Now they are playing important roles in the White House administration. It's a shame how the Trump family uses the US president's office to amass personal profit.

Turkey is another cause for headaches. I cannot believe a German paper would print a whole page of political advertising by Temmuz, congratulating itself on the **Win of democracy over terror on July 15th, day of democracy and national unity of Turkey**. This is certainly a different take on the riots and the failed attempt to overthrow their conservative government last year. After providing data on the dead and the injured, the article praises the private citizens who performed heroic tasks to save their government.

Otto told me he heard from his brother that many Turkish-born European residents actually believe Erdogan is their savior. Sounds incredible to me. After living in liberal democratic countries for decades, those formerly Turkish residents suddenly yearn for a conservative, religion-based government.

The subject of the week was our environment. A huge iceberg, the size of 800,000 soccer fields, broke off in the Antarctic. According to the article, it will take a whole year to melt unless additional large pieces separate. Because it is winter there and pretty dark all day, the scientists have to use special cameras to record the movement of the iceberg.

Just sent another letter to Doris. I'm curious if my political ranting disturbs her or interests her, but I hope it eventually gets her to the point where she will write an answer. Since I only saw her on four visits after she left home at age nineteen, I barely got to know her as an adult and can only imagine what her life might be like. I hope she is financially secure so she can enjoy her retirement. Does Martin live near her? How often does she see her grandchildren?

This week is the Landshuter Hochzeit Festival, a replay of Duke George the Rich of Bavaria to Polish Princess Hedwig's wedding that took place 542 years ago. Every four years, our Lower Bavarian Capital performs a medieval spectacle with knights, body armor, lances, fourteenth-century clothes, and a magnificent pretend wedding. Modern-day street signs are covered in burlap bags, electronics are banned, horses and carriages replace cars. Children in costume have to forgo their fidget spinners, iPads, and skateboards for wooden hoops and jumping ropes. Even the food has to be medieval: lots of meat, cabbage, apples, and bread. No potatoes, tomatoes, or oranges are allowed.

Would I go if I could? I don't know. The festival would definitely be better than the G-20 summit and the riots in Hamburg. In spite of the 20,000-men-strong security force, the police had great difficulties controlling the crowd. The articles I have read so far blame the police, Merkl (because she was the host and because it is her birthplace), the history of the district in Hamburg, and last but not least, the troublemakers from the Black Block, who were dressed in dark clothes and covered their faces to avoid detection.

Despite the smiling faces of the top world leaders during the photograph sessions, little political progress was made during the summit.

Today I have a good reason to cheer; it is a day to celebrate. Lucas came, reported on the graduation ceremony, and proudly showed off his certificate. How I wish I could have been there. On the weekend, his Austrian grandparents will organize a party for him around a great big campfire on a field near their house, as is customary for their clan. Apparently, Wolfgang loved those parties; he met Agnes at one of them.

My appointment with Dr. Kohlberger this afternoon starts out a bit strange. Compared to our previous sessions, he is super friendly, almost disturbingly so. At first, I am pleasantly surprised, but about halfway through the hour, I get suspicious when he tries to sell me on a new experimental program for sex offenders run by a private clinic in Vienna. They claim their treatment reduces all risk to society by eventually stopping pedophiles' sexual attraction to children.

As soon as I start to ask questions about their methods, he points out that I should be grateful to be offered an opportunity to heal my sexual perversion and possibly avoid an extended jail sentence. Hearing this statement puts me on the defensive and I refuse to sign the papers he pushes across the desk toward me. Then I state that I will not consent to any treatment unless I see an official brochure with a description of all the medical procedures, prescriptions, and a list of possible side effects. He gets up, walks out of the room, and slams the door behind him. The whole thing seems set up to intimidate me and get me out of town before the trial.

On the way back to my room, I run into Otto. When he asks me why I look so upset, I tell him about my experience in Dr. Kohlberger's office. First, he is a bit confused, then he remembers something he read a few weeks ago about **phallometric testing** at a psychiatric hospital. They do experiments with child molesters where they expose them at first to pornographic videos involving children and then slowly switch them to adult sex films.

Over a period of time, the pedophile is supposed to lose his interest in children and will watch only adult sex shows. Otto ends with: "I don't recall if they were attracted to the opposite sex or if they are able to lead normal sex lives once they completed the treatment. The experts seemed to be of different opinions."

Toni joins our conversation and adds that he has read the article, too, and confirms that the psychiatric association seemed to be split about how successful the treatment is. Most doctors believe our sexuality is hardwired and doubt that watching videos could have enough impact on pedophiles to switch their sexual attraction from children to adults. Many are skeptical and worry that perverts would be sent back into their neighborhoods believing they were cured and then fall prey to their old urges once they are without supervision and guidance.

The doctors who performed the tests seemed to believe that it was possible to rewire the brain to switch sexual attraction, similar to a student learning a new language. When I ask Otto and Toni if they would volunteer for the experiment if they were in my shoes, both of them shake their heads and say, "Not until I saw test results and spoke to former patients who were cured."

The next day, Mrs. Stiltz drops in to tell me that she has heard about Dr. Kohlberger's attempt to sign me up for this new treatment. She makes it clear that I am under no obligation to do so and cannot be forced to sign documents without her knowledge. Before she leaves, she mentions that a witness has come forward who is willing to speak up on my behalf. She disappears in a hurry without giving me a chance to ask additional questions. Finally, a glimmer of hope.

Later, I hear from an aide that Otto received good news. His review meeting went well and he will be out on early parole soon. While I'm glad for him, I'm also a bit sad because I have come to like him over the last months. Since Toni is also close to the end of his term, I will have no one to hold lively discussions with once they are both gone.

As far as I know, Otto has a supportive family to get him started on the outside and so does Toni. He will have to learn to accept all the help offered in order to turn his life around. Even Lucas will be away if he is able to get a summer job. There is also talk about him going to college in Frankfurt, starting September, which would make it difficult for him to come and visit me here on a regular basis.

The first thing I recall is Mrs. Stiltz yelling and gesturing wildly at a man in a white coat. "Who the hell is responsible for these unauthorized tests on Mr. Griler? Where the hell is Dr. Kohlberger?"

A timid voice tries to defend itself. "The orders came directly from the court. All instructions were followed step by step. I'll get you a copy,"

As soon as the young doctor disappears to fetch copies of the court order with the list of requested tests, Mrs. Stiltz approaches my bed, pulls out her cell phone, and takes photos of the intravenous bag labels and needles attached to my wrist. She checks out my ankles and looks closely at my forehead and scalp. Then she makes calls to order a wheelchair, a nurse, and a medical van to transport me back to the rehab facility.

Her face shows serious concern. "Are you all right? No, don't try to talk if you still feel groggy. Someone will pay for this. Who the hell do you know, who would go to such extremes to stop your trial? Don't worry, I will have you out of here within the hour."

Not in my wildest dreams would I have imagined Mrs. Stiltz could work up such stamina and would go to such great lengths to stand up for my rights. After all, I am—I mean Wolfgang is—known to be a pedophile. How wrong I was to think of her as stodgy and narrow-minded. At the rehab, she requests blood tests to find out what I have been injected with and then calls the police, a lawyer, and the court to request a copy of the test results on her phone. All the while, she sits in a chair near my bed, constantly staring at me as if she is afraid I might get abducted again.

Later, a thin, elderly man, who turns out to be a lawyer, arrives with a stack of papers. They go through them one by one and get more agitated as they scan through them. A few times, one or the other looks at me questioningly, as if to make sure they have the right person in the bed. By the time they reach the last page, their whispered conversation becomes loud enough that I can understand the lawyer's proclamation. "This is ridiculous, this has to be a mistake. Either they mixed up two patients in the private clinic or our client is totally innocent. How strange. In all my years on the job I have not come across anything like this. Even if the court does not allow these tests as evidence, they can't be ignored either."

As soon as the lawyer leaves, Mrs. Stiltz walks over and sits in the chair beside my bed again. "Mr. Griler, we just looked at copies of the tests they did on you. First of all, it was against legal and medical rules to inject you with what could be called truth serums, as if this was an espionage case during the Cold War. Clearly, a person of interest and importance is interested in how much of their shady past you know.

"The strange thing is that the tests were a complete failure. You were not able to answer any of their important questions regarding sexually deprived acts. But—and you can be proud of this fact—you did very well on the standard mental ability tests they performed. You are well-informed in historical and political events up to the year 1989, and then again after February 2017."

Of course I knew the answer to their dilemma but they would never believe me if I told them. Who did Wolfgang know who had such powerful influence to get this court order issued? Is it a connection from the seminary, someone who went on to reach political heights? A co-worker from his government position, who climbed the ladder to lofty success?

According to the book **Chasing the Scream,** this mysterious person might very well be connected to the underground drug scene. Did he recognize a prominent figure in a compromising situation, like a sex orgy? To a point, not knowing is actually a positive thing at the moment, might keep me safe until the trial is over.

Toni drops in to check on me. "Have you heard from your sister? Did she answer your letters?"

When I tell him that I have had no response, he picks up one of the shoeboxes on the shelf, searches through the papers, and then holds out a list of telephone numbers. "Hey, why don't you talk to her right now? You can use my cell phone. I'll type in the number. Here, give it a try."

I hear **Hello** and answer a bit guardedly. "Can I speak to Doris, please?"

The polite voice on the other end turns sharp and wants to know who is calling.

Nervously, I say that I'm her brother and calling from the rehab center. Before I even finish the sentence, an avalanche of swear words and insults hit my ears. Without doubt, this is Martin talking and he is letting Wolfgang know how he feels about him. Stunned, I learn Wolfgang stole all his cash when he visited Rossberg a few years ago. Afterward, he acted like an idiot when Martin wanted his money back.

Tears run down my cheeks as I repeat over and over, "I am so sorry, Martin. I had no idea Wolfgang did that to you. Please forgive him. I am so sorry. I love you so much and would never rob you."

For a moment, there is silence and then Martin asks. "Who are you if you are not Wolfgang? You sound like someone else. I just… I can't remember who."

I hear a click and the phone goes dead. Toni looks at me, astonished. "What happened? That was a strange conversation. I only understood half of it. Was that your sister on the phone? Why did you say you are sorry? What did your do to her?"

There is no way I can answer him. My body is shaking from fright, my arms are thrashing wildly, I lose my balance. Sounds I never knew I could make escape my throat. Toni stares at me for a moment, then runs away. As if from far away, I can hear myself screaming hysterically.

When I come to, a nurse is sitting beside my bed. The moment she realizes I am awake, she bends over me and asks how I am feeling. In my confusion, I keep staring at her until she explains. "You suffered a blackout. Most likely an after-effect of the drugs you have been injected with. Relax, close your eyes for a minute. The current disorientation should wear off in a few hours. We'll keep an eye on your condition for a few days to make sure this doesn't happen again."

As soon as I start thinking about the telephone conversation, my mind starts reeling again. This was much worse than a drug side effect, this was a mind-blowing experience. You see, I never spoke English in my life. Sure, I learned a few words here and there to communicate with the Canadian-born grandson, but I never, ever would have managed a conversation. Wolfgang, on the other hand, was fluent in English.

That is the reason I panicked. If his English-speaking abilities can overtake mine, what else is lurking in my brain? This is not even my brain—only my spirit occupying it.

As I'm stewing in my newfound fears, I suddenly recall instances where I was told that I seem to look different now. A few even claimed they barely recognized me. The question is: how have I changed? Is my mind being overshadowed or is my spirit gradually causing this body to adapt to the new occupant?

This is crazy! I should see any changes as an improvement, thanks to my physical efforts to gain strength and walk again. Why do I get so upset when I look in the mirror and see a face I no longer recognize? Are those really Wolfgang's features, an aged version of the son I used to know? How come I see such a strong resemblance to myself instead, a sick-looking, bald, grey-faced caricature of my former self?

Toni comes running toward my bed, waving an envelope. "Hey, Griler, I have a surprise for you."

As he drops the envelope in my lap, I immediately notice the Canadian stamp. For a moment, I stare at the letter in disbelief, then I fumble with the flap. To speed up the process, Toni takes over and carefully slits the envelope open with his fingernail. Then he pulls out a card and looks at me in surprise. "Hey, it's a birthday card for you. When is your birthday?"

My mind is occupied with the card: best wishes, greetings from Vancouver, no letter, no photo, just a card signed by Doris? Not much, I know, but at least it is a good sign she remembered Wolfgang's birthday. To stop Toni from staring at me, I tell him that my birthday will be in two days, on the 31st.

For a moment, I have the urge to laugh as I realize that I'm actually ten years younger now than when I died. Way to go, Joseph, a whole decade backward. Not many have a chance to start over again.

Really, now you are trying to be funny, what a speedy switch of moods.

Toni gets all hyped about my birthday. Partly because it is also his last day here before his release. All week he has been unusually jumpy. I guess he is nervous about facing the outside world once more. For a moment, I wish I were in his shoes, then reality hits me. What would I do? I have no place to live and lack the financial stability to survive on my own. Even the clothes Lucas brought me from the apartment are shabby and no longer fit me. Mrs. Stilz was kind enough to make arrangement with a charity to bring in a few suits for me to try on. After all, I have to look respectable at the trial in a few weeks.

Otto has avoided me lately and I wonder if I hurt his feelings during one of our lively political discussions. Since we both pretty much share the same leftist opinions, that seems a bit unlikely. Maybe he is the opposite of Toni and seeks quietness to deal with his anxiety about facing life outside these walls again. Like Toni, he grew up in a respected local family and is well educated. His father was an artist who specialized in restoring antique paintings, often in famous churches. From our conversation, I know that Otto traveled all over Europe, even lived and married in Spain in the sixties.

So far, he's never mentioned what happened to his wife or what made him veer off the straight path. He is a few years older than Wolfgang and at retirement age. I do hope things will work out for him this time around. The thought of losing both of them, Otto and Toni, within two days makes me sad. Without our intelligent conversations, my life will be dull and lonely, especially now with the trial coming up and all the misery I will have to go through.

In our last meeting, Mrs. Stilz explained that one of my accusers backed out because she is no longer sure if the abuse actually happened. Apparently, her family received a letter from a Sister Magdalena a few years ago in which she asked forgiveness. She vaguely hinted at being an accomplice in molesting their daughter. The parents remembered this confession when they heard Wolfgang was caught with kiddie-porn on his computer. They delivered Sister Magdalena's letter to the police. Unfortunately, the girl, who is a young lady now, can't remember any details of the abuse.

As I listen to Mrs. Stilz's report, I suddenly know where I've heard that name before. Of course, Wolfgang's second wife Katie called herself Sister Magdalena on the card we found. Before she leaves, Mrs. Stiltz asks me to look for that card and give it to her as evidence. Hopefully, this Sister Magdalena can be located and questioned.

Alone in my room my mind travels back to the eighties. Katie, who now calls herself Sister Magdalena, visited us every weekend to get away from the big-city bustle in Munich. I got to know her quite well. She was a pretty, small-built, energetic young woman with a great big smile or, if you annoyed her, a dark, nasty sneer. What on earth made her think of joining a convent? She seemed to be confident and smart, had an inquiring mind, and would pretty much try anything. Why would she become a nun?

As I remember, she showed no religious tendencies, frequently and fervently spoke out against the church and made fun of pious Catholics in the neighborhood. When our arguments reached frustrating levels we avoided each other. Once in a while we wrote each other letters on the subject of our discontent. Actually they were more like detailed essays about conflicts causing stress between us. One stands out in my memory. She accused me of badgering Erna with arguments about which one of us suffered the most during World War II, a Red Cross Nurse or a soldier. I was totally ignoring the fact that Erna lost a father, brother and all her family possessions.

Once in a while, she became moody and unpredictable, locked herself up in the den or disappeared for days without telling anyone where she was going. Things were not functioning well with the young couple and I suspected that she cheated on Wolfgang. Thinking back, I did not really blame her. He was often short-tempered and distant, difficult to approach and work out problems with.

From what Max told me, things got worse in the house after my death. Katie developed a mean streak, became destructive and violent at times. Still, I find it hard to imagine her molesting a child, but then I never thought Wolfgang was sexually perverted, either. The question is: did Erna have any idea about what was going? No, the most important question is: why would Katie write a letter asking for forgiveness unless she had done something wrong?

My poor wife. I wonder how she managed to cope with such a dysfunctional pair. Must have been embarrassing for her and frightening at times, too. There must have been people who were aware of what was going on. Would Maral have heard rumors? She has not been here to visit me for at least two weeks; neither has Miss Meindl. If they know anything, they most likely won't talk about it because they assume I was part of the scandal and would not want to discuss it.

Lucas did mention a pub where Wolfgang would hang out in the evenings and that he got along well with the proprietor. Did he ever blab or, worse, brag about his perversions with his drinking buddies when the beer loosened his tongue? Did neighbors know that Wolfgang was a pedophile?

When Otto drops in on his last day here, we speak about life on the outside, his expectations for the future, and my hopeless dream of ever getting out. At one point, he talks about his friends from the seminary and mentions an older student named Manfred Stone. Immediately, my parent radar goes off. "That young man freaked me out. I did not want him at my house. I had this weird feeling he might be attracted to Hubert."

The moment those words leave my mouth, I realize my mistake. Otto looks at me, surprised. "You were just a kid, how did you know about Manfred's pedophile tendencies? He was the supervisor of a dorm on a different floor. Don't tell me you were one of the kids from his scout troop. Oh my Lord, you were one of the boys Manfred left in the forest all night, after they blindfolded, stripped, and tied you to a tree, just to teach you guys a lesson on how to respect your elders."

He gives me a questioning stare then goes on. "There were so many rumors going around the seminary about what happened that night. I did not know who or what to believe. You kids are the only ones who can tell that story. If half of it is true, no wonder you are so fucked up. Did your brother ever ask you what happened to you guys in the dark forest? If he was one of Manfred's boys, he would have been there, too; at least he would have known about the incident. I can't believe I totally forgot about that night for all these years. You should write a book about this horror scene from the seminary; it would make a terrific movie, too."

Up to this point Otto had always been friendly and polite toward me, but unspoken boundaries kept us apart. He was in trouble with the law because of his addiction, I was the pervert. Talking about the seminary changed our relationship a notch, I felt compassion in his words when he asked me, "Griler, is there anything I can do to help you get through this, anybody on the outside I could contact for you?"

I was as surprised as he was when I heard myself say, "Do you know a priest I could talk to? I need to talk. I need to tell an unbiased person about my situation. I really do."

Neither one of us had noticed Toni standing behind me, until he asked, "What's the matter with you, Griler? Are you dying? What do you need a priest for?"

He looked so serious that Otto and I started to laugh and, after staring at us suspiciously for a moment, he joined our hilarity. Toni has the habit of popping up at the right moment. This time, our laughter took the edge off our tearful goodbyes. Both promised to visit me once they were settled in their new lives.

CHAPTER SIX:
The Juvenile Influx

WITH LUCAS AWAY ON his summer job, my supply of newspapers has shrunk to a copy of the free local paper and the odd magazines my fellow inmates leave around the common areas. This lack of reading material made me so desperate that I started to go through all the advertising fliers. Here is my opinion: the cost of groceries is shocking. The selection of electronic gadgets, on the other hand, is amazing. The current female fashion styles look promiscuous to me. Young girls wear flimsy clothing, while the boys prefer their pantseats hanging just above their knees. My taste is not strictly age-related, I was also upset when Doris wore a mini-skirt and piled on the make-up.

Ever since my last conversation with Otto, I'm scared to be alone with my thoughts. A few times I attempted to get a discussion going with fellow inmates. After the weather and the food, our common topics are exhausted and I have not found anyone I am able to actually communicate with. This week we had an influx of young men, a miserable bunch. Their behavior is disturbing. They seem to be fresh out of detox and struggle in their new surroundings. The mindless screams, accompanied by yells to s*hut the hell up* in the middle of night, are quite nerve-wracking.

Not even the typewriter offers a distraction. My mind keeps going back to the dark forest and comes up with alarming scenarios of what might have happened to those poor children. How old would they have been at the time? Eleven, twelve, maybe. Now in hindsight, I blame myself for not following my paternal instincts. As a father, I should have asked my two boys questions about the seminary. I should have earned their trust, so they would have felt free to confide in me. After all, I spent several years at a seminary myself and was well aware of what went on behind the scenes. Max lived through the same experience a generation before me.

How many centuries does it take to expose such horrible, vile child abuse? Reading about the Regensburger Domspatzen scandal makes me furious. Over 500 reported abuse cases going back to 1945, first exposed to the public in 2002. How can the average parent even fathom that their children might suffer such degradation and violence at the hand of teachers, guardians, and older pupils? Former choirboys, famous for their beautiful voices, described naked beatings in private rooms, sadistic rituals, physical, mental and sexual abuse.

Therapists who are treating the victims call the boarding school management an elaborate system of cruel punishments mixed with sexual perversion. The accused predators all claim innocence, swear they were following the disciplinary rules and procedures valid at the time and point their fingers at others.

Even the brother of Pope Benedict XVI, who was the head of the choir from 1964 to 1984, is only willing to testify that he knew nothing of the alleged abuse. Cardinal Mueller, who was the bishop of Regensburg from 2002 to 2012, declared that the school structure was revamped in 2011/2012, and only isolated cases of abuse occurred; there was no systematic abuse at all.

After hearing about the Domspatzen case on the news for weeks, I feel a bit intimidated when I'm told by an aide that a Catholic priest is waiting for me in the common area. As I reach for my crutches, it occurs to me that using the wheelchair might give me a more impressive entrance than limping down the hallway on crutches.

A tall priest walks toward me with outstretched hands and greets me with a big smile: "How are you doing, Mr. Griler? I'm Father Kamau, the new pastor in your hometown parish. Let us find a table where we can talk privately."

Trying to squeeze the wheelchair in the space between a chair and the wall gives me an opportunity to hide my surprise before I have to make eye contact with this African-looking priest. Once we are seated properly, he explains that his secretary alerted him to the fact that the prepaid lease payments for the family grave expired. Also, several neighbors complained about our neglected plot, overgrown with weeds and cluttered with dead plants. Politely, he asks who will take over responsibility for the grave while I'm locked up.

His German is almost perfect, only a slight accent gives him away as a foreign-born person. My first thought had been that Otto sent him. To hear him talk about our family grave was totally unexpected. Hesitantly, I explain that I have suffered a memory loss and have no idea who has been taking care of the family plot. Then I admit that I will not be able to pay the fees until bankruptcy has been filed and approved by the courts.

He will have to talk to my legal adviser, Mrs. Stilz. Carefully, he writes down her name before he says with a friendly grin, "Sorry to bother you about the family grave. I'm sure you have more important things on your mind. Are there any other relatives who might help out with the cost?"

Then he shakes his head and says, "Never mind that! How is Lucas doing? Since you moved to Passau, we have lost contact with your family."

His friendly voice is encouraging and I tell him that Lucas is away on a summer job and will attend college in September. When he asks where Lucas has been living while I have been in the hospital, I explain that a friend's family took him in and looked after him. His comment—*what a lovely Christian family this must be*—irks me. I correct him a bit abruptly. "I doubt that they are Catholics.

They are Syrian refugees. Kind and caring people—the father came to visit me."

He seems to be a bit amused by my pointed answer and laughs. "No need to get upset. I was just trying to make a complimentary comment. When you are a priest, your mind automatically goes in a certain direction. How is this family adapting to life in Germany? You know, I was born in Kenya, adopted by a doctor from a Catholic mission at age nine, and basically grew up here. In spite of my excellent German, the first question from strangers is **Where do you come from**?"

That is no surprise to me but I'm a bit shocked that this attitude toward people who look a bit different still prevails. I had assumed bigotry had lost its edge thanks to the many immigrants arriving in the past decade from all over the world. When I voice this thought, he replies, "Sadly, the surge of foreigners brought a lot of insecurity and fear to the surface. I can feel anger, even hatred at times—more often than when I was a school-age lad. At that time, I was treated more like a curiosity than a possible terrorist."

Before he leaves, he asks if I would like him to come and talk to me again. I find myself pleased by his offer, even feel a tiny glimmer of hope that he might actually be open-minded enough to listen and attempt to understand the situation I'm in.

The moment Father Kamau leaves and shuts the door, a buzz of voices breaks the silence around me as if everyone had been holding their breath since he walked in. From the next table come questions like, Who is he, What did he want from you, What kind of religion do you belong to?

When I explain that he is the new Catholic priest in my hometown, they don't believe me. To have a bit of fun with them, I tell them he speaks German well, is friendly, intelligent, and will most likely be a better priest than the last white one we had. They laugh at me and call me an idiot.

This afternoon, I got lucky and found a copy of the *Spiegel*. The article **The Golden Age of Private Prisons** catches my attention. At first, I think this must be a joke when I read that the Dow Jones index is breaking records since Donald Trump's election as president. Apparently even Deutsche Bank believes CXW and the GEO Group to be crisis-proof investments. Those two companies are the largest operators of private prisons in the United States. Trump's new law-and-order policies toward suspected illegal aliens will require an additional 12,000 prison beds, making private prisons more profitable. GEO shares increased in share value from $10.62 to $27 since the November 2016 election. The corporation donated $1.1 million to the Republicans.

How I miss Otto and Toni. This article would have given us such a great subject to discuss. To prepare for the eventual meeting with them, I sit on my typewriter and record the highlights of interesting things I read or hear on the news.

The big subject on the evening news is North Korea with its ballistic missile launches and the United Nations' Security Council's agreement on additional sanctions against North Korea. Their nuclear program will also be a major issue at the Regional Forum of the Association of Southeast Asian nations in Manila.

From the moment I first heard about Trump I found him unpredictable and frightening. Now he found a sparring partner in Asia. Kim Jong-un seems to be an equal match in this crazy war of words involving nuclear rockets with the ability to destroy huge sections of our planet.

I have reached a point where I sit in bed at night, scared to close my eyes. No matter how hard I try to convince myself the creatures of my dreams are only images produced by my anxious mind, I'm deeply afraid of them. The nurse told me that the injection last week must have affected my brain. Her promise that those ugly images will fade away gives me a bit of hope. Still, waking up at night from nightmare after nightmare and then listening to the screaming and yelling around me is seriously messing with my sanity.

Last night, our family grave got mixed into my nightmares. First, I thought I was buried alive, but then it felt like I was sitting on the grave. Various hands emerged, groping around in the dirt, trying to grab me. One hand approached my face and, as I desperately tried to move away, it stopped and started to wriggle the tips of its fingers. Terrified, but also fascinated, I stared at the hand and realized I was watching one of the puppet shows I used to perform for my children. The tips of my long, bony fingers were unusually flexible and bendable, perfect for little tricks and silly antics. Just when I started to relax, long skeleton arms, grimy, grey flesh hanging off them, attacked me.

When I lie in my bed, trying not to fall asleep, I enter a stage where I'm not sure if I'm really awake. Thinking about the trial at night transports me into a zone where I can almost feel Wolfgang's presence. Not angry at me, quite calm, almost like he is attempting to comfort me or telling me he is sorry for putting me in this spot. Just the idea that he might somehow speak about, or replay images of all the bad things he did, horrifies me. In daylight, I believe it would be helpful at the trial to know exactly what I'm accused of, but at the onset of darkness, my common sense and courage fly out the window.

Since I know of the scout troop's horror night in the dark forest, I feel compassion and sorrow for Wolfgang. This does not lessen my anger. An eye for an eye is not something I ever believed in or practiced, especially not when there are innocent children involved.

Part of my dread is the feeling that his spirit is hovering over me, hoping to find a way to influence my thinking. What if he makes me believe his actions were not as disgusting and hurtful as the images my mind created from bits of information I gathered up to this point? Can one ever balance sexual crimes committed against sexual experiences during one's own childhood, using one bad deed to make another seem less evil?

The constant tension in my head is disturbing. This is not a stabbing pain like a migraine but more of a dull heaviness, broken by unpredictable electric currents attacking my forehead. Afterward, I have difficulty collecting my thoughts, my mind jumps from subject to subject, strange thoughts occur to me, nasty pictures flash before my eyes, and I feel like laughing at inappropriate moments. The slightest impolite remark makes me cry—really cry, big tears running down my cheeks.

This is worse than Wolfgang taking his brain back. There seems to be a darker power involved, and messing with me. How can I fight back if I don't know what is happening to me? What if I call Father Kamau and ask him to perform an exorcism? Does the Catholic Church still have priests who are trained to perform that ritual like in the olden days? Probably not! He sounds like a sensible, intelligent forty-year-old and might come up with a scientific explanation.

Mrs. Stiltz certainly would not approve the cost of such an unorthodox treatment. I have not seen her since she rescued me from the hospital, where they gave me the unauthorized tests. She might be busy with other clients of hers; hopefully, she has not forgotten me altogether.

Another whole week without a friendly face, other than George and the priest. Hopefully someone will remember me soon.

Last night, as I dragged myself to the washroom, I heard strange noises while I balanced myself on the crutches at the urinal. When I moved closer to the last stall, I realized that someone was sobbing and trying to muffle the sound. In a muted voice, I called out, "Are you alright in there? Can I help you?"

There was a bit of sniffling and shuffling, then the door latch clicked and a young, tear-stained face peered out at me. Trying not to frighten him, I smiled and invited him to come out, wash his face, and have a sip of water. As soon as he finished these tasks, he stared at me, took a deep breath, then called **Good night** over his shoulder as he disappeared down the hallway.

The incident reminds me that I'm not the only lonely and frightened person in here, but as the oldest one, I should be better able to handle myself, might even want to help those youngsters adapt to this place. Who am I kidding? This scared young man is most likely better informed about Wolfgang's sexual deprivations than I am. As soon as he realized who I was, I could see the shock on his face and his defensive posture. Who is going to trust a child molester, no matter how friendly he tries to be?

A guard interrupts my musings by pushing a partly unwrapped package in my face. Surprised, I open the parcel and find a treasure trove of paperbacks with a note from Otto that he will come for a visit soon. Thank you, Otto. Your present could not have arrived at a better time. My pessimistic mood dissolves fast. Eagerly, I pick up a book and scan the pages.

Just what I needed. An array of fiction published in the last decade. This will give me a much-needed perspective on what is happening in the literary world. But why did he send me *Die Judenbuche*, the only novel written by one of Germany's female poets, Annette von Droste-Huelshoff? Though she lived in the seventeenth century, the same time period as our great writers Goethe and Schiller, her work didn't become famous until the sixties. Her prominence grew with the emancipation movement, when young woman like my daughters searched for female artists and heroes as role models.

This book brings back memories of a teenage Liz arguing with me about the treatment of females in German literature. She described story after story, poem after poem, of heroic men saving their country while their pious, loving wives kept the home fires going, raised healthy children, and nursed the old and poor in their neighborhood. When I countered her with Schiller's "Glocke" and the line **when wives turn into hyenas and delight in causing horror** she became furious and accused me of taking one sentence totally out of context.

I wonder if Doris kept her collection of romantic classic literature, those tiny Reclam booklets that were so popular when she went to middle school. If I remember right, **Pole Poppenspaeler** by TH. Storm, was her favorite. You couldn't find another story to pull at your heart strings like this soppy novel. A pretty Bavarian girl, whose parents travel with a puppet show, falls in love with a young student in northern Germany. The adorable Kasperl, a beloved German puppet, plays a big role in their many adventures.

As the door opens, I look up. A thin young man with curly black hair, shaved on one side, shoulder-length on the other, is staring at me. He turns to walk away, but then changes his mind and says in broken German. "Do you have a book in English?"

"I'm afraid not, but if you write down titles or authors you are interested in, we should be able to order you reading material in English from the municipal library. My friend Otto might also find English-language novels in a second-hand bookstore for you."

He looks at me, confused. I repeat my answer slowly in English, and with what I think are helpful arm and hand gestures, to clarify the message. When I hand him paper and a pen, he writes down five names. I don't recognize any of them but hope they are popular writers or books, which would increase our chances of obtaining them.

Before I have a chance to say anything else, he disappears out the door. Later, when I run into George, the nice guard, I show him the list and ask how I could get hold of these books. At first, he shakes his head at me, then he promises to check with senior staff on how to access the local library.

Moments later, I get called to meet Mrs. Stilz in the waiting room. She watches me closely as I enter the room, sit down in the chair opposite her, and lean my crutches against the wall. Then she stretches out her hand. "Good afternoon, Griler, how are you doing? Sorry it took so long but I had to gather as much information as I could about your case. We never had a child molestation trial that involved so many different aspects, strange circumstances, and unbelievable health conditions."

Then she passes a stack of papers across the desk, and advises me to read them carefully and mark any corrections or objections with the red pen she hands me. Next, she arranges for a small desk to be set up in my cell so I can work in peace and quiet. For a long while, she stands at the door looking at me as I sit in front of the documents. Not in an angry way—more questioning, like she's wondering, *Who the hell is this guy, anyway?*

Her last instruction, before she finally leaves, is to read the medical reports first, then her interpretation of the case and last the names of witnesses who are willing to testify on my behalf.

Working my way through the medical reports is frustrating. I have no idea what certain medical terms mean and no dictionary to check them out. The missing information will have to come from one of the nurses or doctors. Carefully, I prepare a list of unknown words. My fingers get numb often, forcing me to take a break.

As I sit at my desk, squeezing the exercise ball, I replay in my mind what I have just read. Though I can only guess at the meaning of some of my medical conditions, the overall theme in my medical assessment is delusional or split personality.

All the doctors who have examined me physically and mentally provided similar test results but their personal diagnoses on my mental state vary significantly. The one thing they seem to agree on is the fact that I have not shown any violent or perverted sexual tendencies during the periods I was in their care or undergoing tests.

Another point they mention is the personality change: Wolfgang's unpredictable moods, in-your-face attitude, depressed mental state, sadistic and immoral behavior, and unkempt look before the Penny Bridge jump are no longer in evidence. This new Wolfgang is a neat, friendly, calm, eager-to-please but strong-minded man who diligently works to improve his physical shape, shows great interest in current affairs, communicates well, and cares deeply for his son Lucas.

For a moment, I get lost in these positive descriptions and feel proud of myself. Joseph is a respectable human being, striving to make the best of himself. Then I remember that I have Wolfgang's misery and evil deeds hovering over my head. What if I stood up in court and announced, **I am not Wolfgang, but his father, Joseph. My spirit is trapped in his body**.

At best, the court and spectators would think I was trying to be funny. Not one person would ever believe such an outlandish statement. Besides, I would have to discuss this plan with Mrs. Stiltz first. She deserves to be told ahead of time after all the effort she has made on my behalf. Best to get back to those documents. Hopefully, I will find a better solution to my problem.

Even I am a bit surprised by the documented physical changes that have occurred in my brain. Each doctor mentions how the badly damaged parts seem to have healed in various ways and in different sections of the brain. Neither of the doctors comes up with a scientific explanation for how this transformation may have happened. The tests before the operation in the hospital do not match Wolfgang's MIR scans taken three years earlier. The unauthorized tests apparently did slightly blur my mental capacities but, as the nurse told me, a full recovery is expected.

These medical reports would be terrific news if I didn't have to spend the rest of my life in jail. Given this body's age, with a fairly well-working brain, I could expect another ten, maybe even twenty years. What baffles the doctors mostly is the fact that my condition does not fit any current classified medical condition. In my case, a near-death experience switched my personality from one extreme to another.

If I had the option to be honest with those doctors, I could explain to them my fears and nightmares of being overpowered by Wolfgang's spirit. They might be able to write a prescription to stop my brain from being overstimulated. What if this anxiety about turning into Wolfgang confirms the diagnosis of a split personality? Would it mean more experimental treatments or a permanent cell in a mental institution?

Mrs. Stiltz's conclusions are more or less a summary of the doctor's reports and include discussion with me and several people in this rehabilitation clinic. There is nothing that stands out or that I did not know already. As I read the last paragraph I hear my name over the pager with the message to go to the visitors' room.

To my delight, Lucas is waiting for me. He has a day off from his summer job and decided to drop in on me. Grinning from ear to ear he tells me that he has been accepted into an accounting program at a college in Frankfurt. Because he is an out-of-state student, a room near the school will be provided. I'm excited for the great news though I will miss him terribly.

While I was talking to Lucas I noticed the young man who asked me about English-language books. He seems to be having great difficulties communicating with an elderly gentleman. When Lucas leaves, I ask them if they need help. The old man is the grandfather, here to find out why his grandson was arrested. Neither of them can speak enough of each other's language to understand the other. After ten minutes of my translating their questions and answers, the grandfather thanks me and says goodbye.

My English-speaking abilities are apparently excellent. What would the doctors say if I told them about this transfer of knowledge from one spirit to another, or was it just knowledge my spirit picked up in a section of Wolfgang's brain?

Another thought has been disturbing me since my hysterical episode. What if the anxieties and nightmares I experience are inherited from Wolfgang? There is a good possibility the same monsters who frighten me brought him to the point where he felt jumping off the Penny Bridge was his only solution to escape them.

Lucas mentioned a few times that Wolfgang had to swallow an array of prescription drugs every day. Could an interaction of all those drugs have caused hallucinations? How long would residues of those drugs affect a human body? I'm only taking medication for pain—could these pills also contain ingredients strong enough to drive me insane and increase my anxiety?

George, my friendly guard, interrupts my thoughts by dropping a book on my desk. "Here is a book in English, hope you like it."

Out of curiosity, I check the title and author against the five names on the list the young man wrote. It matches one of the authors. Delighted, I flip through the pages and get so interested that I lean back in the wheelchair and start reading. In my other life, I was not much of a reader. Newspapers, political magazines, biographies, yes, but romantic novels, seldom. My wife, on the other hand, loved reading sentimental stuff and sent the kids to stand in line at the library so she could get hold of the newest bestsellers.

Before I have a chance to finish a chapter, I'm called to the front desk. Mrs. Stiltz looks angry and, without even saying hello to me, she snarls, "How can you omit telling me that you are still married to a woman named Sonja? Do you know how bad I look, not knowing such an important fact in your life? All the work I have done to get you on social assistance! Then I find out there is a wife who should be supporting you. How can you take advantage of my kindness like that? What else have you lied about?"

The shock of this revelation hits me hard. How can I be married to this Sonja and no one, not even Lucas, mentioned this to me? Who is that mysterious woman? Too stunned to form my confusion into words, I just sit there. My mind starts reeling around the potential of other secrets coming to light. All I manage to say is, "How come Lucas never mentioned that I married again after I divorced his mother? If this Sonja is my wife, she must have lived in the same place. How can Lucas have completely forgotten to tell me about this Sonja?"

Mrs. Stiltz shakes her head. "Do you really not remember marrying Sonja? Did she never come to see you at the hospital? Where is Lucas—do you have a number where I can reach him and talk to him? This case is just so weird and it's getting way too complicated for my liking."

She heads toward the door, then turns around. "Did you finish reading the documents I gave you last week?"

A bit ashamed, I admit I had problems with some of the medical terms and was going to talk to a nurse or doctor to have them explain them to me. She tells me to do that as soon as possible and to write down my own interpretation of the case as represented by her. Her biggest concern has to do with the reliability of the witnesses. Would they really provide a positive influence during the trial? She advised me to read the list carefully and record all I know about each person on a separate piece of paper.

Concentrating on those documents is kind of difficult with the name Sonja and the words "fourth wife" disturbing my mind. How on earth did Wolfgang meet that woman and how could Lucas not know that his father had married again? The pager interrupts my thoughts. When I get to reception, Lucas is on the phone. In a frantic voice, he asks, "Did you really marry that stupid Sonja? Don't you remember how mad I was when I caught her messing about with my new computer while I was at school? Man, you couldn't even fill out and sign a check, how did you manage to marry her? Boy, this sucks! Mrs. Stiltz is furious and I can't blame her. Do you even remember what a nasty piece of shit Sonja was?"

This is getting worse and worse. With a few words, I explain to Lucas that I have no memory of Sonja or the years in Passau and depend on him to fill me in about that part of our life. He promises to write down the most important things he can recall about those seven years and to come visit me on his next day off. I think, for the first time, I fully convinced Lucas that I really have no recollection of our past life.

Would I fare better by telling him the full truth: I'm your grandfather, not your father?

CHAPTER SEVEN:
Confounding Reports

GEORGE ARRANGED A MEETING with one of the nurses. She was kind enough to go through my list of medical terms and answer my questions in simple-to-understand language. Since I agree with pretty much everything Mrs. Stiltz has put in her summary, I need to correct only a few minor misconceptions, then I quickly sign and date the form.

Describing the witnesses is kind of hopeless as I recognize only a few names. To see Miss Meindl, Maral, Karl, Mrs. Walters, Otto, and Toni on the list of character witnesses makes me happy, though I wonder what Miss Meindl and Maral might be able to say to positively influence the trial. How often did Miss Meindl hear complaints about Wolfgang from my wife Erna? Maral knew him well enough, but from what Lucas said, his father was antisocial most of the time and hated Hansi, her brother. The most important witnesses will be Karl, as a decade-long co-worker, and Mrs. Walters, as the former landlady. They also come from respected local families.

Erwin Jarburger rings a bell. I think his father had a huge dairy farm just outside our hometown. He might have been at the seminary with Wolfgang, but what could he possibly say in Wolfgang's favor? They might have been friends. The name Emil Wegner seems familiar, too. Maybe he was one of Hubert's friends from the seminary. I think they also played on the same soccer team as adults.

Dr. A. Metzger from the University Hospital in Munich is the last name on the list. This name means nothing to me. I will have to ask Lucas about him. My legal team has not been able to locate Sister Magdalena as per Mrs. Stiltz's documents. With our precise bureaucratic system and the current tight security protocols, how is that even possible?

Late in the afternoon, Father Kamau appears at my door with a friendly grin. "Good day, Mr. Griler, how are you doing today? Feel like company?"

"Good day to you, too. Father, did you have a chance to talk about the family grave with Mrs. Stiltz? I'm afraid I don't have a cent in my pocket and I don't want anyone to go after Lucas. He has enough on his plate."

"No, no, don't worry about that, Mr. Griler. I'm here on a different matter. Olga and Elsa Hebner, who used to be classmates of your sisters, approached me after mass on Sunday. They are too shy to appear in court but are willing to write a letter on your behalf. Their brother Felix will testify in court. He did not know you that well because he is much older, but you often talked with him in the pub.

They say since you nearly died in the early nineties you became strange and difficult to deal with. Then things improved for a while when you met Agnes and when Lucas was born. Felix says your happiness did not last long. Losing your brother, mother, and sister within three years hit you hard, turned you into a recluse. Also Agnes having an affair, getting herself pregnant, and leaving you was a big blow to your ego."

"Yes, I know the Hebner family well. I am surprised that they are willing to put in a good word for me. I never got along with their father. We moved in different social circles and belonged to opposed political parties."

Father Kamau looks at me. "From what I heard, you did not move much in any social circles. Most of the time you hid yourself away and avoided all contact except for Lucas. Your own mother had a hard time getting through to you. Felix joked that with each wife your social contact shrank and in the last years they heard and saw little of you. Your ex-wives, on the other hand, seem to have plenty to gab about."

The sentence *since you nearly died in the early nineties* caught me by surprise. I'm anxious to find out what happened. When I ask him, he promises to talk to Felix and get me the details on his next visit. Our discussion is interrupted by Michael, one of the young men standing in the hall. "What's a black man doing in a drab priest frock? Shouldn't you be wearing a brightly colored robe and dance to different gods?"

Instead of putting the big-mouth youth in his place, Father Kamau replies, "I think you are a bit prejudiced. I was adopted by a missionary and grew up in Germany. Never learned how to dance, neither waltz nor tribal dances. What makes you so angry?"

Another one of the boys answers. "Don't take it personal," he says. "He got caught up into the 500-year Luther celebrations. He has been locked up for damaging historical property by nailing copies of Luther's proclamation on church doors. Then he insulted congregation members who tried to stop him and violently resisted the police during his arrest."

Both Father Kamau and I look at the angry young man. He stares back at us. Then he gives us the finger and, clearly pronouncing each word for effect, proclaims, "No wonder you suck up to this pervert. Your church is a cesspool of perverts. A hiding place for senile old pedophiles. You confess to each other and absolve each other's sins. A perfect recycling method aimed at poor kids and the homeless. Roast in hell, perverts."

Each one of the young juvenile offenders in the group gives us a dirty look and the finger. Then they walk away in complete silence.

For a few minutes, we sit there as we recover from this insulting speech. Father Kamau shakes his head. "You know, Mr. Griler. He nailed it. This is a serious dilemma. Every priest gets thrown in the cesspool with the molesters and rapists. We are guilty by allowing the vow of silence during confessions to interfere with the rule of law.

Pedophile priests seek out confessors who they can trust to keep their dirty secrets. Hearing confessions was never my favorite job as a priest, I didn't like listening to parishioners airing their dirty laundry in the booth. The new system of group confessions is more to my taste: think about your sins, regret them, pray for forgiveness and receive an absolution from the priest."

Out of curiosity, I ask: "What would you do if an uncle confessed to molesting his niece? Would you be able to give the parents a hint about what is happening in their family? Couldn't you make an effort to find an opportunity to speak to the child and beg her to confide her abuse to her mother? How can you sleep at night after having heard confessions about sex crimes, spousal abuse, even murder?"

"Griler, as a Catholic who attended catechism classes, you know the answer to those questions. As a matter of fact, tossing and turning in bed was not my biggest problem. Facing a person who has confessed to a serious crime in a public place or a work situation, while attending conferences or social functions, is to me the most humiliating part of my clerical duties as a priest."

To meet someone I despise and put on a sweetly polite front would be impossible for me. I have a big mouth and can't stand two-faced people. To carry other people's dirty secrets on your shoulders, without being able to bring criminals to justice, must be a heavy burden. "Father Kamau, how many priests do you think can listen to a confession and forget all about what they have heard, never think about it again?"

"Well, I can't speak for others, but I can never fully forget or forgive. Seeing a person after many years still brings back the horrible fact of knowing their sinful secret. For me it is rather difficult not to judge, to treat this parishioner like everyone else, as is expected of me. After all, I did absolve each person in the confessional, told them that God forgave them, according to my training as a priest."

"If you feel that way you should be nailing Luther's resolution on the church doors like Michael. Why preach something you don't really believe in?"

We turn our heads to look at the speaker standing in the doorway. It turns out to be the young man I had heard crying in the bathroom. Father Kamau invites him to come in and join our conversation. He introduces himself as Stephan before he says, "You know, Michael has good reasons to be angry. He has been on the street for years.

"Last month, he was nearly killed by a vicious John. Luckily, his friends got there in time and stopped the assailant. The guy who did this to Michael is well known on the street as the dirty old priest. He has been around for a long time. The older he gets, the meaner he gets. Not just in his sexually depraved acts; we are afraid he's ready to maim and kill."

"Stephan, when you say old, how old would you say this priest is? There has to be a way to stop him. Do you have any clues to his identity or which parish he comes from? Do you think he is a pensioner?"

The boy and I look at the priest in surprise. "Father, are you going to get involved and play detective? Even if you find out who he is, how are you going to stop him? Call the police? Who is going to care if a few street kids get hurt, as long as their own children are sleeping safely in their cozy beds?"

Of course Stephan is right. The biggest problem is not the few people who yell at and kick the homeless, but the good, solid citizens, who close their eyes and walk past them without acknowledging their despair and misery. Not many will volunteer to get involved when the victim is a smelly, dirty, big-mouthed and often intoxicated street person. Could Father Kamau actually spur the local police into action if an old priest is involved?

Father Kamau's voice is firm—he is not giving up on this idea. "Stephan, I understand what you are saying, but we will have to find a way to collect enough evidence on this old pedophile to make a charge stick. Do you think any of your friends might be willing to appear as witnesses in court? I will do my own bit of investigation, though I wouldn't know where to begin at this point. Can you and your friends make a list of the streets the old priest trolls, maybe get a snapshot of his face? Make sure you tell your friends not to put themselves in any unnecessary danger. Here is my cell-phone number where your friends on the outside can send me information or photos."

As they say their goodbyes, I ask Stephan if he knows the English-speaking young man, and if he would bring him a book from me. Though he says that he does not speak

English, he promises to find him and give him the novel. "How did he end up in here? Must be a tourist, caught buying drugs or stealing. That sucks, to be stuck here and not be able to communicate with anyone. Bye."

My intent had been to spend a boring afternoon working on the witness descriptions, but then the surprise visitors filled the hours with stimulating religious discussions. Otto would have loved participating in our conversation, so would Toni. Thinking about them makes me miss them once again, but also brings back worries about how they are doing out in the free world.

About an hour later, Mrs. Stiltz arrives and announces, "Mr. Griler, I have bad news for you. The trial date has been moved to the end of October. The judge felt that, until we are able to locate Sonja, it would be better to postpone the court sessions. You know, by finding out about this fourth wife of yours, we opened a can of worms that's hard to sort through. From my talk with Lucas, I got the impression that Sonja must have married you in a secret civil ceremony to get her immigration papers. She cleaned out your bank account by buying clothes and expensive computer equipment. Then she disappeared before she could get caught. For all we know, she might be back in Ukraine by now."

Mrs. Stiltz shakes her head and then questions me on how far I got on my work with the documents. As she reads my statement, she nods. "How soon can you write up your descriptions of the witnesses? There will be a special meeting next week, where all the information we have at present will be pooled, so we can make a decision on how to proceed from there. By the way, we received letters from two sisters, who speak highly of you and your family. Their brother is willing to testify in court as a witness on your behalf. Things are looking up for you."

That must be Olga, Elsa, and Felix from my hometown, as Father Kamau told me earlier. Mrs. Stiltz seems to be pleasantly surprised that there are people in this world who still care for me and are willing to speak up. As we talk about the prospective witnesses, she mentions the University Hospital in Munich and wants to know if I had any recollection of that period in my life. "Griler, you've got to remember if some medical catastrophe happened to you in the early nineties."

As usual, my answer is: "I have no recollection of what happened after 1989."

Then it occurs to me that, at that time, Wolfgang was still married to Katie and I blurt out, "Sister Magdalena would know. She still lived there at that point."

Mrs. Stitlz laughs. "That is very helpful, Mr. Griler, especially since we can't find her. Are any other ex-wives of yours hiding in the bushes? I hope your first wife does not show up with nasty testimony against you."

That was an unkind parting shot, even for a legal aide who has to deal with a frustrating case. Still, I can't get the first two wives out of my mind. Kristie, the first one, was Wolfgang's teenage love. They dated for nine years before they had a big traditional wedding. As far as I know, Wolfgang's drinking caused their marriage to end within a few years, but who knows how many secrets the young couple kept from us.

Though I liked Kristie and am sure she liked me, too, my relationship with Katie—that is, Sister Magdalena—was much more intense, in good and bad ways. I hope she can be located as I have so many questions only she can answer. As I imagine all sorts of scenarios on the theme of Wolfgang's illness that sent him to the university hospital in Munich, Liz comes to my mind. She lived nearby and must have gone to visit him. Then I remember how lovingly she talked about her boyfriend, Franz. He might know how Wolfgang got sick. How can I find this Franz? Does Lucas have his address?

Memories of visiting Liz at the large apartment she shared with friends surface. You had to climb a lot of stairs but the view of the Nockerlberg was fantastic. To live near the Munich city center and see nothing but trees when you look out the window is quite rare. The river Isar was only a five-minute walk away: so was a beautiful botanical garden. At one point Liz talked about taking over the lease for the apartment. What if her beloved Franz is still living at Schild St. 13?

When I was first hospitalized, Lucas promised to find Wolfgang's address book. Looks like we both forgot about Linda, who was supposedly a good friend since she discussed end-of-life issues and funeral instructions with Wolfgang. During my conversation with Mr. Velji about the apartment contents, the decision was made to chuck everything except items Lucas wanted to keep. How could

I forget to ask Lucas about the books, family documents, photos, and address books?

There is also the issue of Lucas moving to Frankfurt and going to college, making the task of sorting through our personal items in the storage space more important. We can't expect the Velji family to keep our stuff forever. When I mention this subject to Karl on the telephone, he promises to talk to his mother and find a solution. Next thing I hear that Toni volunteered to help Lucas. They have already moved all our belongings to the basement and are busy deciding what to keep and what to junk.

The idea of having Lucas and Toni working together makes me happy. The sentimental me can draw up beautiful pictures on how they will bring out the best in each other, until the pessimistic me kicks in and interferes with flashes of them smoking pot in the garden. In reality they are probably just two young guys trying to complete a boring task as soon as possible. Most likely they will come across items with pleasant memories for Lucas and old gadgets that will amuse Toni. Hopefully, they will find an address book.

Last night, there was a big commotion among the young people but I was too sleepy and my body was too stiff to make the effort to get up and drag myself in the wheelchair to check it out. This morning, as I'm getting ready to go for breakfast, Stephan bursts into my room. He is upset and talks so fast that I can barely make out what he is trying to tell me. "My friend Pete was badly beaten up last night and is in the hospital. The police brought in another friend at two in the morning. We know he didn't hurt Pete. That vile old priest did it!"

Stephan helps me button up my shirt, then pushes me in the wheelchair toward the dining room where his friends are gathered, The new boy's lip is cut and bleeding and he has a black eye. He sits there completely distraught, repeating over and over: "Pete and I just tried to help Wiggy. The old priest had him cornered behind a bin in an alley. Wiggy was screaming. That's how we found him.

There was another man in the background. We fought the priest until Wiggy got free. I pulled him away toward the street and told him to run home. The old priest had a hold on Pete and kept hitting him. I went back to help Pete. Then the police arrived and arrested me. They took Pete away in an ambulance. I don't know what happened to the priest. The other man just disappeared during the shuffle before the police got there."

"Why do the police think it was you who beat up Pete? Can't the guy you saved from the priest speak up for you? If you know his name, you must also know where to find him."

They all start to talk at once, each one eager to explain about Wiggy. I find out that they have known him for years. He has Down syndrome, is friendly and happy, has the mind of a preschooler, is about twenty years old now, and walks the same stretch from his home to his day job every morning and evening. For Wiggy to be around after dark is quite unusual; normally, he goes home between 4 and 5 p.m.

Story after story emerged about their interactions with Wiggy. He always said hello on the street. Often, he offered them apples, oranges, cookies, or leftover sandwiches, sometimes even a piece of chocolate or a pop. Wiggy did not like untied shoelaces and warned everyone about the dangers of tripping. If they tied a nice bow, he gave them the thumbs-up sign. When he laughed, his whole body shook or he rocked from side to side. How could anyone even think about hurting Wiggy? They just could not understand how a priest could assault such an innocent young man.

One of the guards comes over to our group and tells us to disperse. One by one they find an empty seat at the tables. I move my wheelchair in a quiet corner and eat my breakfast in silence. This event makes me realize how right Dr. Kamau was when he said the old priest had to be stopped. Breakfast is barely over when a policeman comes in and approaches the new boy. I can't hear what he says, but the boy jumps up excitedly. "There is new evidence. I'm free to go. Thanks for being so supportive. Bye, everyone, bye, Stephan, hope to see you soon."

Stephan comes over and sits down at my table. Michael follows. They think Pete is out of his coma and told them that Ted, that's the boy they arrested this morning, was helping him, not hurting him. Both hope that Wiggy told his parents and that they keep him home for a while until he recovers from his shock. Maybe Ted can arrange with friends to walk him to and from his day job afterward.

Wiggy's parents are apparently well off and, if they decide to press charges, could easily get that priest arrested.

After lunch, Father Kamau drops in and hands me a stack of magazines. "Here, Griler, these should keep you busy. I marked an interesting article and added my own opinion. Read it after you finish the work for Mrs. Stiltz. Next week will be exceptionally busy for me and I won't be able to see you. Take care and don't forget to read my notes."

It is almost evening by the time I finish typing. Quickly, I gather the witness descriptions and put them in the folder with the other documents. As usual, I watch the news after dinner and then hobble on my crutches toward my room. Once I'm ready for bed, I pick up the magazine with the inserted page. At first I'm a bit confused by the message Father Kamau wrote on lined paper: **On the last page you will find two photographs: keep one and hide it in a safe place, give the second one to Mrs. Stiltz and tell her about the incident with Ted last night.**

The photograph is of an old man in a long, black frock. His profile is clearly visible as he leans threateningly forward. One of his hands is on a young man's throat, the other is groping his crotch. This must be poor Wiggy, cowering between the brick wall and a garbage bin, mouth wide open, gasping for air, frightened out of his wits. Quickly, I shove one copy between the documents in the folder. The other one I hide in the typewriter case under a stack of blank paper.

How on earth did Father Kamau get a hold of this photo? Did Stephan's friends on the street get into action that fast? Was one of them the man who disappeared? Did he take the photo? Are there more photos? Question after question goes through my mind, making it impossible to go to sleep.

Tonight it is eerily quiet, no screaming, no swearing, no running footsteps, no telephone rings. Even the aides and security people are silent. Since I know the trial has been postponed, I have been sleeping better at night. This kind of proves to me that Wolfgang's spirit was not trying to take over my brain. My own anxiety was causing the freakish hallucinations and horror-filled dreams.

From Mrs. Stiltz's documents, I got the impression that the main charges against Wolfgang were computer related. Sonja seems to play the main role in the production of the pornographic videos. Wolfgang's diminished mental capacity throws doubt at any active involvement from him.

The identity of the person who was trying to have me committed is still unknown. I have not discovered the slightest trail of evidence or clue of their existence. What am I missing here? From listening to the news and reading the papers, I learned that there is a lucrative underground pornographic industry. The internet enables these sex-distribution networks to function secretly and interact all around the globe.

Just today on the news they were talking about a world-wide child sex ring exposed in Toronto. Those video producers take advantage of the most desperate communities to abuse women and children of just about any age. To profit by selling films of sexual abuse, torture, and murder of children is about the lowest level a human being can reach. Was Sonja part of such a network?

Did Wolfgang unintentionally learn a secret and threaten to expose her?

Did he really jump off the Penny Bridge or did he get pushed over the railing?

CHAPTER EIGHT:
Family Odds and Ends

AROUND NOON, I GET paged and find Toni in the visitors' room. I am really happy to see him after almost a month. He looks neat, much calmer than when I first met him, and seems to be full of energy. "Griler, I brought you a big bag of stuff from the storage area—mostly books, photos, and documents. We also found a few exercise books with your writing and strips of paper with addresses and notes in a bucket. Security is looking through the bag now. The funniest thing we came across was an accordion. Did you really play that thing? Can I have it?"

"Sure, you can have it. What are you going to do with it? Do you know how to play it?"

"Not me, but I have a friend who can use it. I met him at the classes I'm taking at the college. He is a survivor of the street, like me. He has this great idea of starting a street kids' band. He saw a documentary on street kids in Lima, who learned to play classical music and are now famous. He wants to get a grunge band going in Passau. Too bad Lucas is moving so far away—he would have the perfect voice."

"Toni, are you going to join that band? Which instrument do you play?"

He laughs and tells me he is not musical, does not have an ear for it. The courses he is taking are aimed at becoming a compulsive behavior counselor. The plan is to work with street youth, get them motivated to stop self-abusive acts, and channel them into a productive life.

How wonderful; even if he does not complete the courses, he is bound to pick up knowledge and may learn to control his own impulses and not repeat the same mistakes over and over.

That he sees himself as a social worker is great news to me and makes me hopeful he will turn his life around. Though I have no idea what a grunge band is, I think the plan to get street kids together and start a band might work out. Just to have Toni help Lucas with the boring job of clearing out our stuff is a sign of improvement.

When I ask him how Lucas is doing, he jokes: "He was happy to get away from his mom. Between his summer job and the constant nagging at home, he needed a break badly. Lucas calls it a litany of **do this, don't do that**. What exactly is a litany, Griler?"

"It's a prayer. All right, let me see if I can remember. Lord, have mercy on us. Christ, have mercy on us. Lord, have mercy on us. Christ, hear us. Christ, graciously hear us. God, the Father of heaven, have mercy on us. God, the Son, Redeemer of the world, have mercy on us. God, the Holy Ghost, have mercy on us. Holy Trinity, One God, have mercy on us. Holy Mary, pray for us…"

"Hold it, Griler, I get it. A litany is a repetition of the same thing with slight variations. That would drive me nuts."

"Listen, this might actually sound good if you rap it."

I don't know what rap is either, but I used to write jingles and was pretty good at that. The way he repeats his litany with harsh, staccato intonations catches me by surprise and makes me pay attention. Could street kids exploit their own miserable life by transforming it into an art form? Toni laughs at me when I share my thoughts and tells me famous singers and bands have already done so successfully. There is graffiti by street artists all over the city. Nobody pays attention to it.

Maybe street art needs a different approach. Instead of an in-your-face attitude and violent images that turn off the average person, he might consider a peaceful and meaningful art project. Since he is taking courses in compulsive behavior counseling, he might find it a rich source of inspirations and, maybe, just maybe, we could work them into lyrics. As we throw ideas back and forth, we come up with this rant:

stinking bins
ice cold breeze
eyes stinging
shoes soaked

toes freezing
stomach growling
screams of agony
haunted alleys
priest trolling

As soon as I say the last part, I know I shouldn't have mentioned the priest. Toni glares at me and hisses angrily, "What do you know about the dirty old priest?"

Now I have no choice but to explain about Ted, Pete, Stephan, Michael, and Wiggy. The moment I mention Wiggy, Toni totally freaks out. "What the hell are you talking about? The dirty old priest hurt Wiggy? What a bastard! Man, if I get my hands on him."

The people around us are staring and I have a hard time calming him down. As quickly as possible, I make him understand that there is a plan underway. Any crazy, spontaneous action on his part might wreck the plot to get the old priest arrested. I tell him to wait a few days, then visit Mrs. Stiltz in her office. My instructions force him to listen and he relaxes. If he wants to get involved, she will explain to him how he can help. By the time he leaves, he actually has a grin on his face.

When I get back to my room, I find a large, bulging pillowcase on my bed. Anxiously, I pull open the cord and peek inside. Then I take out anything that might be used as an address book. While I'm opening one of the notebooks, a photo drops on the floor. Sitting in the wheelchair, I try to pick it up, carefully balancing myself as I lean forward.

A hand shoots into sight and grabs the photo before my own comes even close to it. As I look up, I'm shocked to see it is Otto who came to the rescue.

My first reaction is spontaneous. "Otto, what are you doing here? I did not expect to see you in this room ever again."

Otto grins. "Just a small setback. A couple of months' penalty. I got caught drinking while on curfew. A small relapse, if you will, not a total falling off the wagon. Who is the old-fashioned lady in the photo?"

When I say **It's my mother**, he looks at me in disbelief. "Come on, Griler, don't mess with me. Hubert's mother looked nothing like this old lady.

I saw Toni talking to you in the visitors' room. How is he doing? Did he bring that big bag of papers and photos?"

So, this is no strange coincidence to see both of them on the same day. Otto knows about Toni's visit and appears in my room within minutes. I explain to him that Toni helped Lucas sort through our stuff. Today he brought me an assortment of books, documents, photos, exercise books, and loose notes I might be interested in.

Otto still looks at me strangely. "What were you two doing, laughing and joking? It looked like you were planning some mischief."

The idea that Toni might become a youth social worker seems to amuse him, but as I tell him about the street band his friends are planning, he shakes his head. When I mention that I have no idea what grunge and rap music are, he laughs at me. "Man, where were you the last twenty years? Did you get your head stuck in the sand some-where? Even if you don't like modern music, you must have heard about it at one point or other. How about the Green River Band, Nirvana? Grunge is a hybrid of heavy metal and punk."

Quickly, I change the subject to the lyrics we were playing around with. The title **Litany for street kids** appeals to Otto. He worries though that the word litany might offend too many Catholics. I promise to discuss the issue with Father Kamau next time he comes to visit. Immediately, Otto apologizes for not keeping his promise of asking a priest to come and talk to me. "How did you find a priest with such a foreign-sounding name?"

"Actually I didn't even look for a priest, he found me. Father Kamau is the new priest in my local parish and he came to tell me that the lease payments on the family grave had expired. Turned out to be a nice man, great to have an interesting conversation with. After you and Toni left, I felt pretty much alone, no one to discuss things with. Father Kamau is open minded and actually volunteered to help the young delinquents who arrived after you left."

"Griler, you amaze me. Looks like you are actually getting involved in other people's problems. Never thought you would be making friends with the clergy. I heard from Mrs. Stiltz that your trial was postponed. She sounded pretty positive, told me there is a lot of new information coming out that might be helpful to you. Even I can tell that you are more relaxed and your body seems to be more flexible, too. Good for you. Maybe some of that positive vibe will rub off on me."

We spend a pleasant hour talking about current affairs and world news. He tells me that he lives with an old cousin in Altweg and how fed up he is with local politics. Last week, he attended a meeting regarding the Syrian refugee reallocation and was shocked by the many protest signs. Then he got angry at the district council, who consistently shut down questions from the crowd and overrode each and every one of the resolutions the village council members brought forward.

The community was willing to accept fifty refugees, the district delegation forced over 100 on them. Seems unbelievable—that is almost ten percent of the village population. No wonder the local citizens are worried and getting angry.

The federal government leased the land and provided old shipping containers. They are being restored as living quarters and stacked to resemble an apartment building. The village has to find places for the children in the local school, distribute government paid supplies, welcome the newcomers, and organize police, fire and ambulance services. Otto says: "I checked out the site and was pleasantly surprised how nice the containers looked. There is no way you can call the refurbished containers an eyesore."

Without thinking, I tell Otto that I know Altweg well. It is only a thirty-minute bike ride from my hometown. At least I did not tell him that I was born there. Am I ready to confide in Otto, announce to him *I'm not Wolfgang.*

I'm Joseph, his father? Am I dropping clues unintentionally or on purpose? What could I say to convince him I'm not Wolfgang but Joseph? If he were my age, not Hubert's, it would be easy by talking about war experiences only a former soldier would know.

After Otto leaves, I have another look inside the bag. Among some paperback books, I find an envelope addressed to me. In it is a letter from Lucas. He apologizes for taking such a long time and promises to send me more information. His memories of Oma (grandmother) are mostly flashbacks to playing games with her in the garden or in her apartment. Looks like Lucas loved our old place, had a treehouse in the backyard and a big swingset.

He wrote that Liz came to visit Oma once in a while. She was a lot of fun, chasing him down the hallway, pretending to be an ape. Hubert visited seldom and, when he did, he brought his girlfriend along. Oma did not like her, but Agnes became friends with Clementine. The last time Lucas saw Daniel was at Oma's eightieth birthday. There was a big family fight and they lost all contact. Only Doris speaks to all family members. Lucas promised to send me his address in Frankfurt as soon as he is settled in.

Daniel—that was my other grandson's name. How could I forget! From what I read, Lucas had a pretty happy childhood in my old home, except when his parents were fighting. Most likely they vied for his attention and spoiled him rotten. Luckily, he turned out well in spite of their behavior. The sentence **Doris speaks to all family members** irks me. What about me? If she is in contact with Lucas, why does she ignore my letters?

There is no space for all the books, so I decide to stack them under the bunk bed. Looking at the titles, I wonder whose books they really are. A few I recognize from our bookshelf, many are bestsellers, others look like they came from Katie's collection. The Isaac Singer books are definitely my wife's. Otto might like to borrow a few books to pass the time.

I decide to stack the pages in Wolfgang's handwriting and tie them into bundles for now, except those that contain names, telephone numbers, and addresses. One of the last things I pick up is a business envelope. On closer inspection, I realize that I'm looking at draft legal documents, a last will and testament, and burial instructions. The representative was named Linda Winter. The papers are outdated and from before Wolfgang sold our house, but the contact information for Linda is helpful.

In another envelope are photos, mostly from our family album, until I come upon horrid photographs of Wolfgang. Frightened eyes are the only sign that he is still alive under this scaly looking skin, in this extremely thin body, covered with large dandruff-like flakes. The tube in his nose and that he's hooked up to several intravenous bags suggest a hospital setting or a scene in a horror movie.

When I turn one around, I see, written in Katie's handwriting: **after rehab photos, University Hospital, July 1993**. Just looking at the photos makes me sick to my stomach. What on earth happened to Wolfgang? I select a few of these photos and put them in the folder for Mrs. Stiltz, as documentation of Wolfgang's health problems in the early nineties.

She arrives the next morning and, before I hand her the folder, I explain the reason why I included the photograph of the dirty old priest, as he is known on the street. When I tell her that Toni would like to help catch this pervert, she laments loudly, "What makes you think I want to get involved in this plot? Don't you think I have enough work without participating in unpaid investigations?"

Quickly, I try to think of an answer that might change her mind. "What if you enlarge the photo to the size of a poster and tell Toni to put copies up in prominent places? Other victims might be encouraged to come forward. This priest may have molested children for decades. They will be of all ages and social groups and might be more convincing than the street kids. You don't have to get involved. All complaints would go directly to the police."

I omitted to tell her where I got the photo. At this point, I don't want to mention Father Kamau's name and accidentally blow his cover. He is going to have enough hurdles in his investigation if he is trying to get at church records. Stephan and his friends are eager to help, but they would easily get overexcited and overreact if they came face to face with this pedophile priest.

Yesterday, when I offered them books from my under-the-bunk-library, they looked at me as if I was incredibly stupid. Michael was the first to open his mouth. "Griler, who do you think you are dealing with? Look at us!

How many of us do you think have the mental capacity to get through those old classics? Our reading materials are comics."

From the doorway comes Otto's voice. "Maybe your lack of education is part of your problems. Would you be interested in taking free German lessons from me for about two months? We could borrow a few of Griler's books and I could help you get through them. Looks like I have nothing better going here and one or the other of you might actually learn a few new words."

After I introduce them to each other, Stephan is the first one to volunteer. He also wants to know if Otto would tutor the English-speaking man, who needs to communicate in German. Since day one he follows everyone through the daily routine and then sits quietly in a corner. According to Michael, he must have read the book I got him a hundred times. Otto agreed to help though, as he admits his English is out of date.

The lessons must have been successful because several books disappeared and I saw little of Otto and the young men. Actually, come to think of it, nobody dropped in on me the rest of the week. On Saturday evening, while I am eating my dinner, the mood in the common room somehow changes. I feel tension in the air, but also an undercurrent of excitement, a touch of suspense, like when people gather to watch fireworks. There is no talking. They all seem to be waiting for a signal to go off.

Halfway through the evening news, I get my answer. The photo of the dirty old priest, blown up to poster size, appears on the screen. A reporter introduces Wiggy's parents, who are furious that they had to learn about the attack on their son from a poster. Why had the police not told them about the assault on their child, and why had nobody warned them about letting their son walk to work by himself?

A police spokesman blames it all on a bureaucratic error and announces that the clerk who was responsible was fired as soon as her failure to notify the parents came to light. When the reporter asks if any other victims came forward, the police spokesman answers reluctantly. "None of the claims have been verified at this point."

The rest of the news is drowned out by howls of laughter and high-fives. Stephan is jumping up and down. Security enters and shuts down the jubilant group. Even as they sit there quietly, their faces shine with excitement. They have won their first victory. This is a huge step in getting the dirty old priest off the streets.

My goodness, Toni must have been awfully busy hanging those posters. How I wish I could tell the guys that he did all that work. Or do they already know? They must have known. Why else would I have felt that turbulence in the air?

A bit later, Otto stands at my door. "Well, Griler, inter-esting developments, what an exhilarated news audience. Did my German lessons get those guys suddenly interested in local politics? Have you got any idea who that priest is?"

"Not really. All I know is that he is well known on the street as the dirty old priest. They are scared of him and worry he is going to kill someone, if he has not already done so."

To change the subject I ask him how his German lessons are going. I admit that I was surprised when the whole group decided to further their education. Then I wonder aloud if there is a chance to get free classes organized, where they would earn credits, maybe learn a trade or go to college when they get out. Otto promises to talk to his brother, who used to be the principal in a private school.

Even at night, when the lights are off, I can still feel a slight vibration in the air, a positive vibe giving me the feeling of hope—for myself and the young men. Otto puzzles me. He seems to be fine with being locked up again, but had no problems on the outside either. Being such an intelligent man, one of the most open-minded and calm people I know, why does he drink if he knows he can't handle it and will be arrested if drunk?

Was he one of those people who strive too hard to meet their own high expectations, who push themselves too far and then crash? Coming from a famous artistic family, he may have given up at the start, believing he wouldn't be able to surpass his father's or a sibling's achievements. There is no use speculating about Otto—maybe one day, when he is ready, he will tell me what made him give up on the struggle for a better life.

Two weeks after this exciting evening came a shocking announcement over the pager. "Griler, a Sister Magdalena is here to see you."

Ignoring the taunts and stares in the hallway, I wheel myself to the visitors' room, anxious to talk to Katie, my former daughter-in law. Since I have no idea what she looks like now, after almost thirty years, I head in the direction of a figure dressed in a light brown, ankle-length hooded habit, in the style peasants wear in old church paintings. The woman I meet seems to be just as confused as I am. Her first words are hesitant. "Wolfgang, is that really you? You look so different."

"Hello, Katie, good to see you again. Your new look in this sack-cloth outfit is hard to reconcile with the pretty young woman I remember. Thank you for coming, I'm really glad and have tons of questions for you."

"What's the matter with you, Wolfgang? You talk weird. You sound like your father. What happened to the grumpy, moody ex-husband I remember? When did you start being polite and friendly? That priest, who called out of nowhere, told me where you are and that I'm wanted by the police as a witness to your sex crimes. I figured I'd go see you first and find out what is going on before I report to the local police."

Now, this is interesting—the police couldn't find her but Father Kamau did. He turns out to be a great detective. Looks like he managed to scare her enough without telling her much. Now that I have a chance to look at her, there is no doubt this is Katie—a slightly older version, but a well-kept one. This new religious lifestyle seems to agree with her.

Impatiently, she interrupts me. "What's going on, what did you do? What has this got to do with me? Stop staring at me!"

"Hold your horses, Katie. I did not involve you, you did that yourself by writing letters of apology to people without actually explaining what you did to them. You sent one to a neighbor, saying you were sorry for being an accomplice in molesting their daughter."

Katie has visually shrunk into herself. Meekly nodding at me, she quickly changes her tune. "What happens now? How can we fix this? The letters were written right in the beginning, when I chose to become a nun, as a way to purify myself. To amend for past sins and clean the slate. What did you tell the police?"

Hesitantly, I explain to her about having no memory of the nineties. She is the one who will have to tell the police what happened. This seems to frighten her and I'm surprised at her reaction. The Katie I knew would have come up with a plan, made up excuses, fought like a tiger to get away with it. This meek woman acts like a helpless nun.

Out of curiosity, I ask her which order she belongs to since I have never seen a habit like hers before, especially not on a woman.

"Come on, Wolfgang, you know all that. Your mom helped me shorten the tunic and the sleeves before I moved to the convent. Don't you remember how you walked in, saw me in the habit, and started to laugh hysterically?"

Again, I explain to her that I can't recall anything that happened between March 1989 and February 2017. "My first memory is of waking up in the hospital from an induced coma. The rest are bits and pieces of what people have told me about my past. The last thing I recall about you is the moment you told us that you signed the lease on a health-food store in Arnfeld. You expected to get rich by selling nutritious snacks to wealthy spa clients. Looks like that idea did not pan out."

"Are you trying to be funny? This is so strange. You are supposed to be Wolfgang but you talk like your father. Do you really have no recall about what happened with, darn it, I forgot her name. It was all harmless, really. After you came back from the university clinic you were listless, tired, and totally useless in bed. To entice you a bit and get you sexually excited, I invented a game with the girl. When she dropped in, I asked her to strip and dance for us. I rewarded her with a few coins or little gifts. That's all. Didn't work anyway—nothing got you sexually excited, at least not while I was around."

Now this is a strange turn of events. The supposed sexual predator is unable to perform. I wonder what Dr. Kohlberger would have to say about that. The big question would be what would the police do with this information since the girl can't recall anything. As things stand at the moment, Mrs. Stiltz definitely needs to talk to Sister Magdalena.

Since I have no guarantee that she will actually turn herself in to the police, I decide to make sure of that and wave over a security guard. "This is Sister Magdalena, the police are looking for her."

Katie screams at me. "You idiot, why did you do that? I haven't done anything wrong."

Calmly, I look at her. "Exactly, Katie. All you have to do is tell the police. This is the only way I can make sure you will do that. They have a lot of questions for you about Wolfgang, what you know about his sickness—physically, mentally, and sexually."

When she yelled, she sound exactly like the Katie I knew. As she demurely walks away with the guard she has turned back into Sister Magdalena. In the hall Stephan walks up to me and says. "Griler, I heard you made a nun so mad that she screamed at you and called you an idiot. Why would you do something like that?"

"What would you do if your second ex-wife showed up suddenly, dressed as a nun? Now imagine how you would feel if you had no memory of ever being married to her? I cannot refute anything she says because I don't know what the truth is."

Stephan stares at me, not quite believing that I'm actually telling the truth. Then he decides to let this subject go and updates me on the newest information regarding the dirty old priest. The papers are reporting on women of all ages who claim to be his victims. The police still call the sex crimes *just allegations* at this point, while the Catholic Church is suspiciously silent.

Since I have not heard from Father Kamau for weeks, I'm a bit worried that he might have been caught while snooping in filing cabinets. Because I don't recall telling him about my ex-wives, he must have gotten his information about Sister Magdalena from another source, most likely in my hometown.

As a priest he was obligated to show the photo to a representative of the bishop first, to give the church a heads up on a most likely embarrassing event coming up. That conversation would have been complicated if he was not willing to expose the photographer.

Mrs. Stiltz dropped in for a few minutes this morning to warn me to tread carefully. "The photo you gave me stirred up a hornet's nest. The whole town is buzzing at this moment. Tell your young friends to be patient. The old priest will be locked up for sure, but it will take a while for all the evidence to be sorted out. There are too many high-profile local people involved and the police have to proceed with caution."

A few days later, an Asian-looking gentleman walks up to me and introduces himself as Father Lau, Father Kamau's legal representative. My frightened expression seems to amuse him. I relax when he tells me that my friend is fine. The diocese lawyers felt it was best to relocate Father Kamau until the case goes to trial. When a spot opened up in a diaspora parish a few days ago, he was appointed to that position. He left this morning to begin his work there. I'm totally shocked. "The diaspora? They sent Father Kamau back to Africa? That's crazy, he can't even speak the language."

Father Lau nearly chokes laughing. "No, no. This diaspora is a small town outside Berlin, where all the Protestants are. He will be quite safe. You know I would like to meet the young man called Michael, the one who nailed Luther's proclamations on church doors."

Across the room Otto is sitting with a group of students, explaining something to one of them. Stephan and Michael are busy reading. As we approach their table they look at us suspiciously and Otto turns to me. "What is it with you, Griler? Where did you pick up another foreign-looking priest?"

Stephan is worried. "Did the bishop send you? Are you trying to shut us up and stop the investigation on the dirty old priest? All of us are going to fight you, if it kills us."

After quieting the group down I introduce them to Father Lau, who explains. "I used to be a priest but extended my studies to become a lawyer. At the moment I hold a position with an organization that deals with priests who work in foreign countries. Father Kamau does not really qualify for our legal aid because he grew up in Germany and speaks the language fluently. Only his darker skin sets him apart from the local clergy."

"What happened to Father Kamau that requires legal aid? Don't tell me he got in trouble for helping the street kids get one of the worst sex offenders out of the back alleys."

"No, no. Can I call you Otto—I don't know your last name. Father Kamau is fine, he was relocated to a new parish outside Berlin until the trial of the priest you just mentioned. That was strictly for his protection and organized by our legal team. Kamau is the one who wanted me to talk to you. You see, there might be an opportunity to put pressure on Catholic social services departments.

We may be able to work out a deal that would compensate those who have been assaulted by the aforesaid priest."

Father Lau explains to us that Pope Francis is working with the World Church Forum to investigate child abuse claims. They will also provide former victims with schooling, housing and monetary assistance, to help them recover and hopefully lead a safe and healthy life in the future. In spite of his mispronunciations and his thick accent, not one of the guys snickers. All pay close attention, most of all, Otto, who is delighted with the turn of events and keeps asking question after question on the subject.

At the end of the discussion, Father Lau approaches Michael. "You know, Michael, our group was impressed when we heard about you. Your action was a good reminder that we are all doing the work of God, which is not always in the best interest of the Holy See. People like you, Michael, are the true Christians. They stand up for what they believe. Your message is especially important this year, as we celebrate the 500-year anniversary of Luther's proclamations."

The next day I replayed that conversation over and over in my mind. First, I was pretty amazed by the open-minded Father Lau, then I started to remember instances in my last life, when I admired other clergy. Having to listen to boring sermons every Sunday at High Mass for five decades makes you appreciate a priest who actually preaches well enough to make your ears perk up. Controversial subjects made the members of the parish think, disturbed their religious complacency, and encouraged them to open their minds to new ideas.

In my generation, being baptized a Catholic basically put you in a private club, anything outside the church was considered diaspora. We were the only ones who held the keys to the Heavenly Gates. This attitude slowly changed after WWII, partly due to shame, once the horror of the Holocaust went public, partly because immigrants of different religions, fleeing the east blocs, mingled with the mainly Catholic Bavarian population.

When Doris was around fifteen, she came home from a three-day prayer retreat in an abbey, raving about one of the speakers, Pater Theodor. She was floating in a spiritual pink cloud, convinced she was meant to become a nun, to forsake a sinful life and follow the golden path to heaven. Knowing her, I had no doubt that these religious ambitions would not last very long. At the same time, I believed that Pater Theodor had greatly influenced her spiritual outlook. I admired him myself.

He was one of the few priests who spoke up against Hitler and paid for his bravery with several years in a concentration camp. The church was silent while the Nazi atrocities took place, then turned Pater Theodor into a hero after the war. There were priests who supported the Nazi regime; the majority did not. They were afraid to speak up, were scared of being arrested. Instructions from Rome to defy Hitler's evil doing might have given them some backbone, pushed them to break their deadly silence.

One of our liveliest religious discussions around the dinner table took place in the early fifties. My mother started it by quoting parts of the sermon of Father Strasser, an old-fashioned, half senile priest. The theme was the obedient Catholic wife, a common enough subject. Our family quarrel erupted over one sentence. I don't remember the exact words, but Father Strasser basically proclaimed that **a wife had to drop whatever she was doing, whether it was cooking, cleaning, or nursing the baby, to do her wifely duty**.

The women vividly protested such arrogant instructions and ranted at the church's obsolete stance on birth control and the violence against females associated with oppressing behavior. If you combine forced spousal sex with the lack of financial assistance to large families who follow the church's abstinence rules and produce unwanted babies as the withdrawal system fails them, you create a recipe for poverty and misery. Hans and I stood no chance of winning this argument.

For once, wife, mother, mother-in law, and sisters-in law were all on the same page, united in their womanhood.

Now it seems so silly when I think of all the chauvinistic stuff that came out of my mouth. Hannah, Liz and Katie were constantly battling with me about female and male roles in society, often walking out on me, and leaving me to stew in my own discontent. Hubert's wife Hannah was by far the most intelligent and ambitious one.

When Lucas wrote about Hubert's visits with his girlfriend, I fully understood why my wife was upset. After all, we all loved Hannah and gladly accepted her as a family member. Clearly, Hubert had suffered a mid-life crisis, which is quite understandable when you consider that his wife was the only doctor in the family. To bring his love affair into the home of an elderly mother was like rubbing dirt in her face. As you get older, you want things to stay calm, you expect relatives to be nice and understanding, not bring friction and worries into the short span of life you have left.

CHAPTER NINE:
Exposed on Twitter

LAST MONTH, I WAS constantly busy, first with the trial documents, then the pillowcase full of stuff to sort through, and, of course, all the tumult regarding the predator priest. I was not even aware that Lucas had not been around for a while until I received a letter from him. He has arrived safely in Frankfurt, writes of his comfortable dorm room and how he is learning to adapt to college life. At least he felt guilty about not having a chance to say goodbye, as planned.

Compared with the wildfires in British Columbia, and Hurricanes Harvey and Irma and the devastation they left behind, my life is pretty safe here in Passau. In early September, our TV stations dealt mostly with the trauma in Houston and surrounding areas, then focused on Florida as the hurricanes passed state lines. The damage in Cuba, one of the first areas hit by Hurricane Harvey, received little coverage in spite of the extensive destruction. Of course St. Martens and St. Thomas got headlines in Europe because they are favorite tourist destinations.

At present, the lack of US emergency response in Puerto Rico after Hurricane Maria is on the news, especially since Trump got involved. Watching him throw supplies at people who lost just about everything they ever owned, are hungry, and have no electricity, telephone, or medical services, is humiliating. I have come to think of that orange-haired president as inhuman or so mentally disturbed that he can no longer see past his own nose.

Despite all the politicizing before the federal elections here in Germany, the outcome itself was pretty much indecisive; the rise of the alt-right, on the other hand, was deeply shocking to me. At present, our country is still waiting to see which parties will form a coalition. That Merkl only got a minority of 238 seats, followed by the socialists with 148 and the AfP with ninety-five was a bit unexpected. The other three parties managed to nab the balance of the seats—the FDP: seventy-eight, the Left: sixty-six, and the Greens: sixty-five.

All the confusion this distribution of seats caused makes a two-party system in the United States look like a sensible arrangement. This current fuss about political correctness is starting to corrode our freedom of speech by putting too much weight on social laments by Twitter users.

Just recently, I read an article about worldwide greed, violence, and idiocy jeopardizing the middle class. Housing has become too expensive for families with half-decent wages, while the cost of average living requirements has risen rapidly. Citizens who are squeezed too hard will eventually push back. History provides enough proof with past riots and revolutions.

Last week, I watched a documentary and could not believe my ears when I heard Evangelical fanatics in the States are still preaching that God is punishing our planet with hurricanes, wildfires, and wars because of Western societies' sinful behavior. Brings you back centuries to when witches were burned and innocent people were killed because of a murderous, religious, eccentric madman acting like a warrior of God.

A local newspaper article blamed Merkl's failure to get a majority government on the diesel emissions scandal. The mayors of thirty German cities expected a government pledge to fight pollution and improve their cities' poor air quality. They feel she has been too cozy with the powerful automobile industry and are angered that she did not speak up against those major automakers earlier.

My political pondering is interrupted by a visit from Otto. After his greeting, he sits silently on my bunk. He is obviously upset; his body is tense and he avoids eye contact. Then he takes a deep breath and blurts out, "Griler, I have to tell you something, OK? Promise to stay calm, OK?"

When I nod, he continues. "Toni was coming to see you this morning, but then he talked to an elderly lady, who was sitting on a bench across the street. She looked nervous and asked him if he was going to visit someone inside. When he said yes, she told him that's why she was here, too. Only she did not have the nerve to go in.

"Toni told her that it would probably make the person inside happy to see her. She got up, looked at him, and mumbled something that sounded like she didn't even know who he was… Maybe he was her brother… Maybe he was her father.

"To calm her down, Toni asked if he could take a message for her to someone inside. She answered a bit absentmindedly, 'Tell Mr. Griler, I'll be back in a couple of weeks.'

"Then she looked up at the windows, shook her head, and slowly walked away.

"Toni came in and asked to see me. He thinks it was your daughter. What the hell is going on here, Griler?"

This is certainly not the scenario I had imagined when I thought about telling Otto the truth. As so often in the past, Doris—if it is really her—is forcing me to play my hand. At this point, she is probably not ready to face me. Knowing her, she'll collect the facts, then slowly work her way through the confusion associated with my person. At least she came. And, as she said to Toni, she will be back. How can I explain this to Otto?

"Hey, Griler, come on, say something. I deserve an explanation!"

"Otto, I have been thinking about telling you the truth for some time but was afraid you would not believe me. I'll start with what I know. In February, I woke up from an induced coma, not knowing who I was. No, that is wrong, I knew that I was Joseph Griler's spirit, and that I died in

February 1989. What I didn't know was whose body I was in, not until I picked up bits of information from nurses, doctors, and visitors."

"Griler, that's crazy. Where was your soul the last twenty-odd years? Well, at least now a few things I found suspicious about you actually start to make sense. If you were dead, where were you all that time and why did you come back?"

"All I remember is drifting through a bright tunnel and then suddenly being ejected into a greyish, cloud-like atmosphere. Nothing but emptiness, filled with thoughts from all kinds of people. First, I panicked because there was no hiding; everyone knew what you were thinking. Then the spirit of my father Max showed up and taught me how to hang around pleasant thought groups. I believe we were in some kind of limbo, a punishment for low-level sinners, a place for souls with unfinished business.

"Max told me he had traveled back to earth several times. When my daughter Liz showed up and told me that Hubert and my wife had died before her, I kind of freaked out. Then Max's mother verbally attacked me, called me a wimp and a loser. I grew so angry that I spiraled out of control, got pulled into space, then beamed back to earth. After a moment of blissful floating, I hit something lumpy and got sucked into deep waters by a strong current."

"So, the old lady was right when she said to Toni that she is not sure if you are Wolfgang or his father. This is weirder than science fiction. How can anyone believe you? What would have made your daughter suspicious?"

"Otto, I don't know. I suspect my letters were not in Wolfgang's style. As a matter of fact, from what I have learned in the past months, he might not have been capable of writing letters at all. Even Katie, alias Sister Magdalena, kept asking me why I talked so strangely. Why I sounded more like her father-in law than her grumpy ex-husband."

"Just how will you explain your situation to everyone? Why would you want to go on trial for something you did not do?"

"The way I see it, no one will believe me. The only way I can avoid a trial is by pleading insanity. I did not come back to earth to spend my time in a mental institution. But most of all, I need to find a way to help the victims. Maybe a sincere apology and jail time served will soothe a bit of their pain.

"Believe me, I have spent numerous nights thinking about this. Since Wolfgang is not around to make amends, I will do it for him. If only I knew how bad his depraved acts were—the police will not give me any information. Everyone expects me to know what Wolfgang did, since they think I *am* Wolfgang. There is no way of getting around this. That's why I wanted to talk to a priest, to confess my dilemma and ask for advice."

After Otto leaves, I start to type out our conversation. Then I read it over and try to make sense of what I wrote. I can't imagine what a stranger would think of my story. My list of questions I need to ask Doris, if the elderly lady Toni saw was really her, grows steadily. It consists mostly of memorable moments between the two of us that will be proof that my spirit is really occupying Wolfgang's body. Only I, her father, would know about those events.

Sleep evades me as memories of my children flash through my mind. My best times as a father were when they were little. I loved telling them stories, taking them on walks and bike rides. In the summer, we spent every sunny afternoon on the river Rott, splashing and swimming. The boys learned how to ski on the local hills and the girls skated on the frozen creek. What an idyllic picture!

In reality, Hubert and Liz were good in sports. Doris was a goofy klutz. That girl hated physical exercise, partly because she was overweight, partly because she was unco-ordinated and ashamed to try.

To make up for her lack of athletic skills, Doris acted the goofball. Clowning around on the ski hill, she lost control of her sled and hit a cement wall. She came home, blood running down her forehead. Once she skated on the creek into the roped-off area and crashed through the ice with one leg. By the time she got home, her foot was frozen into the boot. At twelve, she rode her bike too fast into a curb, hit the gravel, wiped out, and broke her arm.

Yet she was the only one in the family who came to visit me in Munich on school holidays. She took the train by herself, walked to the construction site, and helped me hand out drinks to the laborers. After work, we played tourists. An old couple, long-distance relatives, usually invited her to stay overnight with them.

Doris was the family ambassador, the first to volunteer to visit an uncle or a cousin, to deliver a present or pick up a forgotten item. Twice a year, without complaints, she rode her old bike, on a gravel road, for three hours, to Fuchsberg. How proud I was to hear my relatives compliment me on my friendly and polite girl.

Then Doris became rebellious. I caught her at age fifteen at a dance hall. My heart beat wildly as I stared at her slow-dancing, cheek to cheek, with the most popular guy in the district. She glared back at me and kept dancing even closer to him. It took a lot of nerve not to hit the young man and pull her off the dance floor. It took a lot of effort to smile and politely converse with him before I marched her home. By the time she finished school she had such an active social life I barely saw her on the weekends I was home.

How angry she got when I used her Munich apartment as the mailing address for the jingles I wrote. Acting all grumpy, she would drop the return letters and samples I had received on the table. I was worried about her living alone in the big city, barely eighteen years old. She got boiling mad if she caught me spying on her.

Yet, she was the only one to visit me every evening while I was undergoing tests at the University Hospital. Doris also defended me when I refused to volunteer for further experiments. The rest of the family made me feel like a coward.

Then she left for Canada and I barely got to know her as an adult. Her four visits, three years apart, were much too short to find out what her life was like, what kind of a woman she had grown into. Besides, all the attention was centered on her children, and I was pleased to see that she really enjoyed motherhood.

Of course I knew she was avoiding me, did not want to be asked any questions. Should I have persisted, pried a bit harder? Why was I so afraid that I might push her even farther away?

I never saw Doris again, despite my begging letters to come.

The thought, that I may have been still alive when Wolfgang molested children fills me with fury and disbelief. How could I have been unaware that I lived with a pedophile? Or did I? Why did I not protest at the first accusations? Did I harbor suspicions before I was confronted?

My son hurt little girls. Not only one. I understand this much now. Any child coming to our house might have been his victim. Was Wolfgang a predator? No, I'm sure he would not have gone out and searched for prey. He was much too lazy and undecided. He would have acted only if an opportunity arose. Couldn't say no if he was tempted, maybe stoned or drunk enough to override any sense of decency.

Were we so blind in our ignorance that we never noticed any odd behavior?

Did he never slip up, give us clues about his pedophile tendencies? He and Katie came home most weekends. She obviously knew or she would not have invited a neighbor's girl into the house to perk up their sex life. How many people were aware and never spoke up? What did they say behind our back?

How could I not notice if friends looked at me sideways or treated me differently?

This morning, after a sleepless night, my head is heavy and my eyes are sore and crusty. Absentmindedly, I hobble toward the bathroom on my crutches. When Stephan stands in my way and stares at me, I ask him to move over. He grins at me. "Hey, Griler, who are you this morning, the father or the son? Have you really come back from the dead? Into your son's body? Man, that is so cool. Your name will be all over the news."

"Please, Stephan, not now. Let me go to the bathroom. I'll talk to you at breakfast."

The thought, that my situation might be news material had not occurred to me and scares me. Now I wish I had not blabbed to Otto. When he joins me at the table, I ask him why he told Stephan. Otto looks surprised. "Oh, no, Griler, he has not heard that from me. He found this information on Twitter and, according to what I heard, your secret is getting a lot of controversy. Once you post something on Twitter and it catches on with the followers, it spreads like wildfire."

Patiently, he explains to me how fast rumors and facts multiply on Twitter, how difficult it is to distinguish the truth from lies. Just last week, in the midst of a Hollywood sex scandal involving a famous producer, a movie star put on Twitter that she was abused and challenged other woman to come forward using the hashtag *metoo*. Millions of women from all over the world posted their own abuse stories.

We have barely finished breakfast when Father Lau comes into the room. Our juvenile gang surrounds him, most likely to update him about the article they read on Twitter. He laughs at them. "Cool it, Stephan. I have read the article. Mrs. Stilz tagged me. Good morning, Mr. Griler, how are you adapting to being a Twitter star?"

The moment I mention that I have not read the article, he pulls out his phone, pushes a few icons, and hands it to me. With mounting anger, I read under the heading **Wolfgang Griler**: child molester claims he transitioned from a different human, has no memory of crimes, speaks in voice of father. Hashtag: you believe this? Tick yes or no.

"Hey, look, Griler, so far you have over 187,000 no's and fifty-three yeses. Let's all vote guys. Hands up for no. All right, more than half. Hands up for yes. Only three? What about the rest of you? All undecided?"

Father Lau looks around the room. "Well, the undecided may be the smart ones. There is a lot of evidence coming out. The whole situation is quite strange and difficult to explain at this point. Several handwriting experts are working on the case. Even the KGB-type, unauthorized tests Dr. Kohlberger ordered support a total personality change, if not a different spirit occupying Wolfgang's body."

"Dr. Lau, are you suggesting Mrs. Stilz wrote this article?"

"No, no. The premature public exposure was quite a shock to her. She met with her team as soon as she found out. Hopefully, they have time to prepare before the media knocks on her door, looking for a story. When I left her office she gave me this letter for you.

OK, guys, let's leave Mr. Griler alone with his mail. Let's move over to the empty table over there. How are the grammar lessons going?"

Otto sees me fumbling with the flap and comes back to rip it open for me. Anxiously, I pull out a letter, typed on Mrs. Stilz's office letterhead. There is no greeting, but the first sentence provides the reason.

> Can't face you, can't even manage to address you. Deep down I know, I can feel, that you are not Wolfgang. Still, I can't fully accept it yet.
>
> The exposure on the internet came from Marianne Kuntz. She cornered me on the way to the train station and told me she would force you to confess.
>
> Fathers Kamau and Lau trust you, so does Mrs. Stilz, but not to the same extent.
>
> We are trying to find Wolfgang's old hard drive.
>
> Talked to Agnes's sister, who worked with him at a singles' club in Schatting.
>
> Found Lisa and asked her questions.
>
> Going to spend a few days with Helga. Lucas turned into a charming young man.
>
> Until later, I hope. Doris

My heart beats like crazy. I feel like laughing and crying at the same time. To know that she is actually trying to help me, despite her mixed emotions, fills me with hope. She still loves me. Honestly, I'm such a whiner! She always loved me, we just didn't get along.

To know that she is spending time with Helga relaxes me. They have always been more like sisters than her and Liz. Thinking of Liz, she would get such a kick out this whole situation, but would not get involved. She would expect me to clean up my own mess.

If Hubert were still alive, he would distance himself, would try to avoid this sex scandal and protect his child at all cost. Hans always thought my oldest son was a bit of a snob, but I understood this strife to move up into higher society, to mingle with the privileged students he had envied at the seminary.

I still don't get how **Twitter** works, can't figure out how Stephan found this post so fast. There must be a connection, but who tagged him?

What a long day! Nothing catches my interest. Stephan tried to get a conversation going, so did Otto. On the news the uncontrolled wildfires in California, destroying towns and wineries, gets my attention temporarily. The win of the young upstart Kurz, who formed his own political party in Austria and then won more votes than the established parties, upsets the liberal governments in Europe.

For a while, I listen to Otto, Stephan, and Michael discuss the news. My thoughts keep drifting back to that post on Twitter. Without thinking, I say aloud. "Stephan, who sent you that post on Twitter?"

Embarrassed, he stares at the table. He does not want to give up his source. That means it is someone I know, most likely Toni. So how would Toni have found out? Doris wrote it came from Marianne Kuntz, but who sent the post to Toni? In her letter, Doris also said **Lucas turned into a charming young man**. That proves she has been in contact with him and most likely still is. Maybe Lucas knows this Marianne Kuntz.

Stephan is sitting there, head bowed and silent. Otto speaks up for him. "Let him be, Griler, he meant no harm. He just repeated what he read. We would have heard it sooner or later. Michael and I talked about it earlier on. We both think that now, while your case receives so much publicity, there will be a scramble to expose other offenders. Pedophiles everywhere will be in panic and fear of being outed. The Regensburger Domspatzen scandal centered on one institution; this will affect all rungs of society."

Then Michael adds, "Griler, I'm really glad for you that your daughter met with Mrs. Stilz. Toni was worried she might not come back again. She also showed up at Mrs. Walters' house for a visit. They all sat in the backyard, asking questions and answering them as well as they could, sharing what they knew about your case and writing down what they thought might be helpful."

This is maddening—my daughter is talking to everyone but me. Even Fathers Kamau and Lau seem to be in contact with her. Would be great if I could listen in on the conversations between Doris and Helga. My sister-in law can't stand me. Will my daughter defend me?

A flashback to the eighties hits me. That's exactly how paranoid I was in my senior years, always afraid of bad things being said behind my back. I was well aware of my miserable moods, my whining for attention, unjust accusations and their effect on others. Once I got caught up in those negative thoughts, I couldn't switch them off.

After lunch, I join Otto and Michael's table in the common room. They are discussing authoritarian regimes, which are getting too oppressive, throwing democratic principles out the window. Otto believes our passive, permissive society has created a desire for authoritative leaders. Michael figures the huge amount of information we receive on a daily basis is often contradictory and misleading. The general population is getting confused and longs for a leader to tell them what to think and what to believe.

There certainly has been a shift in several countries. Erdogan in Turkey is jailing human rights defenders. Orban in Hungary has reversed liberal legislation in order to bring the judiciary under government control. Maduro in Venezuela is locking up opposition leaders. That madman Duterte in the Philippines has suppressed free speech and authorized extrajudicial killings of alleged drug dealers.

Then there is North Korea, which has been a dynastic totalitarian dictatorship long before Kim Jong-un, who is taking this single-party state to new heights of surveillance, arbitrary arrests, and atrocious punishment for political prisoners.

As I listen to the group talk, I realize how well matched Otto and Michael are in their political, environmental, even religious beliefs and ideals. They probably share a similar background, a good education, and a free-spirited personality, though age-wise they are a generation apart. Stephan grew up differently. You can tell he is struggling with the grammar lessons and has a pessimistic outlook on life. He is a fighter and most likely struggled from a young age to provide for himself and defend himself.

At one point, Stephan looks at me. "Toni thought it was funny that you have those two old ladies trying to help you. He was surprised they got along so well. He said it made him appreciate his grandmother, to see her talk about issues he would never have dared discuss with her."

"What do you mean, old ladies? I am a lot older than they are. Mrs. Walters is in her eighties and Doris is over seventy now. I was born in 1914. I am—I can't believe I'm bragging about this—I am 103 years old."

After a moment of confusion, they all start laughing, hooting, and clapping. Security walks toward us and tells us to disperse. Later, Otto comes to my room and we rehash our earlier discussion. The Twitter message might turn things around for me—hopefully in a positive way. He doesn't think the two old ladies, as Stephan called them, would be able to make a difference. Still, he gives them credit for trying.

The next days were uneventful. On Saturday, around noon, I get paged and told there is a visitor waiting. Anticipating a visit from Doris, I wheel myself excitedly down the hall. As I look around for an elderly lady, a tall, slim, young man walks toward me. "Hello, Mr. Griler? May I introduce myself? I'm Daniel. Doris told me about your situation. I came out of curiosity. You keep staring at me. Do you know who I am?"

I'm stunned. This is Hubert's son, no doubt about it. That smile is just like Hubert's. The eyes though, those piercing, dark blue eyes, are Hannah's. He is amused by my shocked silence. Finally, I manage to speak. "This is a dream come true. From the moment Max told me about you, I wanted to meet you.

"Not one of my visitors ever spoke about you. I began to doubt you actually existed, until Lucas mentioned that he had not seen you since your Oma's eightieth birthday party. I'm delighted to finally meet you. Can I call you Daniel and shake your hand?"

Grinning, he nods and extends his hand, then changes his mind, comes closer and gives me a great big hug. "Hallo, Opa."

For the next hour, we exchange questions and answers. He came against Hannah's wishes, out of curiosity, intrigued by Doris's story. At this point, he is not sure how our relationship will develop—he has to consider his mother's feelings. She passionately hates Wolfgang, since he did not speak up against Agnes. He let her and that crazy Clementine insult and shame her.

Daniel remembers playing in our beautiful garden with Lucas, riding his scooter in the parking lot and chasing him around the soccer field across the street. Grandma spoiled them with cake and cookies. In the summer, she picked juicy strawberries in her garden, sprinkled them with sugar or topped them with ice cream. Charley, his cat, followed them around the house and yard.

When I prod him with questions about girlfriends, he keeps mum, just grins at me.

Hesitantly, I ask him. "Daniel, what made you accept me as your grandpa without asking questions? Doris is still struggling with it."

He smiles at me. "How can I explain this? I sensed it the moment I saw you. I just knew you are not Uncle Wolfgang and speaking to you confirms this. He always seemed distracted and gave the impression that he didn't give a damn about you or anyone else. Well, except for Lucas—he clearly adored little Lucas.

"You, on the other hand, give off a friendly vibe and listen to my words. If Doris saw you face to face, she would be convinced, too. At this point, she is too worried about the trial and what will happen to you. Once that is over, you two can have a long talk together, get to know each other again. Don't worry, Opa, I'll be back soon."

Long after he is gone I sit there, totally transfixed by my surprise visitor, filled to the brim with happiness and excitement. I cannot make myself move. I want to stay in this space and replay our friendly dialogue, dwell in the pleasant feelings and emotions.

Otto is the one who approaches me and breaks the spell. "Hey, Griler. We are all waiting in suspense to hear who this mysterious visitor was. From the suit and tie he wore,

I would guess he is a young legal aide, Michael believes he is a representative of the church, and Stephan thinks that he might be your new psychiatrist. Now, come on, tell us, which one of us guessed right?"

"None of you! The visitor was my grandson Daniel, Hubert's boy."

CHAPTER TEN:
Surprise Visitors

NOW THAT I'M OPENLY calling myself Joseph and no longer pretend to be Wolfgang, the way my fellow inmates treat me has changed from hated pedophile to nutcase and liar. Strangely, being called crazy does not bother me as much as I had feared. Those who were friendly before seem to accept my new identity, almost as if they suspected that there was more to my memory loss than I told them.

Since Daniel's visit, I have had no contact with the outside world and I'm beginning to worry about the progress of my court case. Finally, on Wednesday this week, I received a legal letter advising me that October 26th is the date set for the preliminary hearing. At least I will know in ten days what new evidence my team has come up with.

Why is Doris not coming? She must know how badly I want to talk to her. Is she staying away on purpose to hurt me? Where is she, anyway? Why does she not want to face me?

Last night, Otto told me that he does not have to appear at the preliminary hearing. He has already given Mrs. Stilz written statements, a positive one about our friendship here in the institution, and one from when he knew Wolfgang at the seminary. As we talk, he admits: "I'm nervous because my time is up at the end of the month. How will I survive without drinking to blank out my misery? No one trusts me anymore. I have disappointed them too often."

At great length, we discuss the options he has on the outside. Otto is nearly seventy. What kind of assistance will he get from family, friends, and social services? During our conversation, he points out that I will be even worse off. Aghast, I listen to him as he explains that, if the judge decides I'm Joseph, I will no longer receive Wolfgang's pension and won't qualify for my own because I died in 1989. All I can expect is a measly welfare check, hopefully with a bit of disability pay thrown in because of my physical condition.

The rest of the afternoon I sit on my bunk and reminisce on the past, our old house, friends, and acquaintances. Of course, there is no going back home—the house is sold, strangers made their home there. None of my buddies are still alive. Ms. Meindl and Maral have been kind, but that is the extent of what I can ask from them. My grandsons are too young and can't afford to look after me. The rest of my family is in Canada. Helga made it clear that she would not get involved in my affairs.

A few days later, Toni comes for a visit. This is a new Toni; he is full of himself, confident, and energetic. His college classes are going well, he loves living with his grandma, he is actively involved with the street kids and collecting evidence on the dirty old priest. I keep looking at him, delighted that he has found a cause that excites him and gives him hope for his future. I can imagine how much Mrs. Walters will enjoy his company and their lively conversations.

My thoughts veer back to the present when I hear him say that Doris is back in town, talking to Mrs. Stilz. Both will be at the preliminary hearing. Toni wants to know how I get treated since I announced I was not Wolfgang but his father. Like Otto, he had wondered who I really was, but blamed the memory loss for my old-fashioned attitudes and missing knowledge. Then he tells me: "Lucas is lonely in Frankfurt. I'll visit him on the weekend to cheer him up."

I barely have a chance to wheel myself back to my room when I get paged again. This time, Ms. Meindl happens to be my surprise visitor. After a friendly greeting, she hands me a little parcel with the words: "I thought this might get your mind off your troubles in the coming weeks. How are you holding up? Are you really Joseph, not Wolfgang?"

To my delight, I find a copy of my book of poems in the package. I tell her how happy this little book makes me and ask her questions about people we both used to know. As I suspected, there are not many of my old acquaintances left. Among other things, she tells me that a nice couple with a large family bought our house. They keep the building and yard neat and tidy and get along well in the community.

When she is ready to go, she looks me over carefully, than gives me her opinion on my situation. "You know, I'm glad I came to see you. I really believe you are Joseph now. You talk like him and discuss old friends from my generation that Wolfgang would barely know, never mind care about. Good luck at the hearings next week."

In the afternoon, Michael barges into my room. He is out of breath and all hyped up. He just manages to say: "Griler, have you heard from Father Lau? There is a rumor going around that the dirty old priest did not show up for his court date. What if he is hiding out in a secluded monastery? The police will never find him. Maybe they sent him to some secret abbey in South America and he will disappear there like so many Nazis after the war. We got to do something to keep him locked up."

"Michael, from what I have heard, this is an old man. I doubt that the church will go to great lengths to hide him. He would never be able to leave the EU, not with the tight security at the airports. Besides, with all the sex scandals going on, the church's lawyers have no choice but to produce the old priest for the court hearing, unless he is sick or mentally unstable."

Before I can complete the sentence, he interrupts. "That's just it, Griler. How are we going to get justice if a doctor declares him senile or too frail to stand trial? Remember the photo, there is nothing frail about the way he pinned Wiggy in the corner behind the bin. Believe me, that old man is strong, his grip is lethal. Why do you think we are so scared of him? He might be a priest, but he is brutal, dirty, and vile."

After a while, Michael calms down a bit and our conversation turns toward a plan to find out what happened. Maybe Otto talked to Father Lau recently or Stephan has heard rumors from the streets. I tell him Toni was here earlier and never mentioned the disappearance of the old priest, only that he was gathering evidence from the street kids. Obviously, Toni did not know about the missed court appearance.

At that point in our conversation, I'm paged and told to go to the visitor's room. Once I get there, I look around for a face I might recognize, still hoping Doris came to see me. After a minute or two, a pretty young woman approaches me. "Is that you, Wolfgang? You look so different. Doris thinks you are her father. Just had to come and see for myself. You really have no idea who I am, do you? Come on, Wolfgang, I'm you sister-in-law, Ingrid, Agnes's sister. Remember, we met at a singles club in Schatting. I still regret the day I introduced you to Agnes. This is so sad. You can't remember me at all, can you?"

Now this is a totally unexpected turn of events. One of Lucas's favorite aunts is here to see me and it looks like she knew Wolfgang quite well. I can't help asking: "You are so young—he didn't harm you, did he?"

She looks at me and without hesitation, answers, "No, he never touched me. When he drank too much he became a bit lecherous and talked stupid stuff. Usually, it took only a stare, a few times a firm **no** or **_get lost,_** to get him to back off. Wolfgang was never pushy or nasty—a bit leering and salivating, maybe, if a sexy patron attracted his attention. What am I doing, talking to you in third person. Is this some kind of game you are playing?"

"I'm afraid I really can't recall anything of Wolfgang's life after 1989. That's the year I died. Doris mentioned you in her letter. Looks like you know her. Lucas said he likes you very much. Though we are no longer related, I'm still glad to meet you."

Ingrid continues. "In the beginning, Wolfgang and Agnes tried hard to make their marriage work for Lucas's sake. Both families felt that they were not a good match. I know my sister is a silly goose. She can get on your nerves, nattering constantly, nagging and whining. I can understand why Wolfgang disappeared at every opportunity. He kept playing the depressed, disinterested, stoned man. She looked elsewhere for action and excitement."

"I get the impression that you liked him. Didn't his drinking and drug problems bother you? From what I know, he struggled with this addiction since his teenage years. Were you, Agnes, and the rest of your family not aware of his alcohol and drug abuse?"

"How could I not know? That's how we met. The singles club in Schatting was operated by former users and kept in business by a wild mix of music lovers and well-meaning citizens who tried to get the homeless off the street. I'm the youngest in a strict Catholic family that turns into a clan of obnoxious drunk adults on the weekend, joined by freeloaders from the area."

Like my other visitors, Ingrid seems to accept me as the father of Wolfgang; our conversation simply confirms Doris's earlier report.

Back in the cell, I reach for my book of poems. Within an hour of reading, I'm emotionally torn and uncomfortable. The writing itself impresses me but I'm disturbed by the way I turned silly grievances into woeful laments. What did Max's mother say? That Max and I only care about our own feeble emotions, even turn them into soppy dramas? Sadly, my poetry proves her right.

For the first time, I compare my current state of mind with that of the spirit who spiraled through a light tunnel in February of 1989. Looks like I not only adapted to new technologies but also gained tremendous spiritual growth in the last months. Just think of the physical pain during my hospital stay, then the mental agony of being treated like a pedophile, the nightmares and the fears of the unknown I have suffered.

Great waves of relief and gratefulness wash over me. I have now reached a mental state where I feel I can handle my physical challenges and the aftermath of Wolfgang's criminal behavior.

Best of all, I have friends, people who care about me and who will support me next week when I badly need them. While I was in the hospital, I heard horrible, negative things about Wolfgang and was all alone in my despair. How I hated this rehab when I arrived, but I have to admit, it forced me to reevaluate old habits, beliefs, and attitudes. Of course, Lucas, Toni, Otto, George, Father Kamau, and the gang of young juveniles helped by challenging my old-fashioned attitudes and forcing me to adapt to my surroundings.

Is that the reason why I want Doris to come, to impress her with this new me? The essence of our relationship is spoiled by friction. She can't accept me the way I am, made it clear I was not the father she dreamed of. This new Joseph is a changed man and I need her to like him. Does she have any idea how desperate I am, how badly I need her to respect me?

Come on, Joseph, don't go down that alley again. Don't give what she thinks of you so much importance. She is an old lady now, not a rebellious teenager.

George comes in holding out an envelope. "An old lady dropped this off for you, Griler. How are you doing? You haven't been to the gym all week. Might be good to get rid of some of the tension while waiting for the hearing."

Again, there is nothing but my name on the envelope. In my eagerness, I struggle to rip open the flap and stare confused at several pages of what seems to be two unrelated stories. The first is titled **The Vott-Mill**. Eagerly, I start to read.

For years, for decades, I've been hanging around this mill, the weir, and the brook, looking for something, probably my childhood. At least, that part of my childhood

that is imprinted in my mind: Vott-house, mill, weir, brook, and the outhouse on stilts, poop splashing in the cesspool below the weir. Certain is that these memories are intertwined with Herbert's death.

Herbert was my best friend, until he and I fought for Peter's attention.

I'm stunned. This is a hard hit from the past. Only Wolfgang could have written this story. It is true, Herbert was his best friend. Half of the story is about their parties, soccer games, driving around, meeting girls, going to Peter's eighteenth birthday celebration. Shortly after a fight between them, Herbert was killed in a motorcar accident. Wolfgang blamed himself, figured his friend would still be alive if he had been the driver. Peter suffered serious injuries but his father carried the guilt of letting Herbert drive his car. Mr. Vott refused to lend the boys his truck because he felt Herbert was not responsible enough.

Because of Herbert's death, my memories from this time are much more vivid than they would have been if we had grown old together. I still can see and feel the semi-darkness inside the mill. Konrad, their helper, had intense light blue eyes staring out of his white, flour-dusted face. Mr. Vott, tall and solidly built, ordering Konrad and Herbert around in a loud and deep voice, full of authority. The strange clanking, squeaking, banging, swooshing sounds of the machines and equipment made a mysterious background noise. How happy I was when Herbert finished his chores and we were able to escape his frightening father and the mix of wheat bran and grease smell in the mill.

A few years ago I saw a different side of Mr. Vott, a gentle Opa playing with his two small granddaughters. Not a trace was left of the man I feared as a child.

How well Wolfgang described the mill, though I was surprised that he was afraid of Mr. Vott. The man was always friendly and kind. Well respected, too, but then he may have had to be firm and loud with Konrad, who was mentally slow and a bit hard to manage at times. Most people were scared of Konrad, not of Mr. Vott.

Lately, old stories are pushing to the foreground again, most likely triggered by the three deaths in my family. I can't deal with three deaths within three years, can't handle the emotions. Herbert's accident rose to the surface and a strange force pulls me toward the now abandoned mill. The big gate is boarded up but I approach the weir from the other side of the brook.

Water is no longer cascading down the weir, only a small trickle runs down on the side near the old water wheel. I sit there for hours absorbing the atmosphere, ruminating in old memories, trying to connect with Herbert's spirit.

Poor Wolfgang, why didn't he talk to someone? Where were his friends? Did his wife know how depressed he was, or had she left already? He writes that people expect him to get a grip, deal with his loss, get on with his life, but he can't, he just can't cope. How terrible. To lose his brother, mother, and sister in such a short time. He was afraid and lost, felt all alone.

Today, the second day of spring, I climbed through the nearby gully in search of the first flowers to photograph with my new camera. That's when I found the trail along the brook, no longer used by children, overgrown with reeds and weeds. This is where we cut the strongest reeds for arrows when we played at being American natives. My name was Rattlesnake, Herbert was Old Grizzly. One year we built a raft and nearly went over the weir in the spring, when the brook was high, beginning to flood. I wish I had an opportunity to look inside the mill, take *photos of the old machines and equipment, now most likely rusted and covered in dust. Herbert's family is long gone.*

He ends the story wondering if photographs of the mill would put an end to this strange attraction that area has over him. He hopes that this pull he feels is only a small distraction, a way to stop thinking about the deaths in the family he can't deal with, the losses he can't accept.

Is he holding conversations with Herbert's spirit to cover his loneliness and pain? How did he manage to live in our house filled with memories, good and bad, of a whole lifetime? This must have been the reason he hated Rossberg so much.

Tears run down my cheeks as I sit there, wholly in the grip of Wolfgang's story. Suddenly, Otto grabs me by the shoulders. "Wake up, Griler, you have been paged a dozen times. Come on, wipe your face, I'll push you to the visitors' room."

I see her immediately. It's Doris. She looks upset and approaches me slowly, giving me time to pull myself together. But I can't stop crying.

"Papa, I'm so sorry I dropped off Wolfgang's stories. I should have talked to you first. You do need to read them in order to get an idea of Wolfgang's mental state before the hearing next week. Which one did you read?"

"The Vott Mill. I'm so glad you came, Doris. My mind is reeling with questions and full of confusion. Are you still angry at me? Is that why you did not come in before?"

"No, no, Papa. I'm not mad at you, I just could not face you in your misery the years before you died and now in Wolfgang's body. Papa, I have suffered pangs of guilt ever since I read your journal. I should have tried harder to truly accept the positive influence you had in my life. Over time, I did grow up, but I'm still in the habit of disappearing when I can't handle a situation.

In no way can I cope with the fact that Wolfgang abused children. Knowing that he did that killed a part of me, the part that loved him. Sure, I talked to him, I tried to be polite, but that's it. There is the little brother of my childhood and then there was this pedophile who is my brother."

While she talks, I have an opportunity to look her over. I'm shocked how much she looks like Erna. I kind of expected to see a modern version of my Mama. Her eyes are the same strange green color but they are calm, not frantic and anxious like my mother's. She returns my stare. "Seeing you helps me get over my fears of having to deal with Wolfgang's perversion. This may be his body before me, but you have changed the expression on his face. Papa, his body looks younger than the last time I saw him."

When I ask how long it was since she last saw Wolfgang, she tells me about her visit three years ago, describes Mrs. Walters' house and the beautiful yard. Wolfgang was in good shape physically but had severe short-term memory loss, kept repeating the same old conversations over and over, wrote notes to himself and then forgot to read them.

She said the best way to talk to him was while walking. Physical activity seemed to stimulate his brain. They hiked up to the castle, visited the graveyard where my step-brother is buried, climbed the hundreds of steps up to the pilgrim church Maria-Hilf, and roamed the hills on the Austrian side.

Their conversations went well as long as she did not touch on subjects Wolfgang did not want to talk about. Then he clammed up, claimed memory loss.

As I prod for more information, she tells me that he had a room full of stuff from the house, boxes stacked against the wall, odd things lying on top. She remembers seeing the old lampshade Erna had woven herself and Lucas's old toys. All the shelves in the bedrooms and living room were crammed full of books, though he could no longer read.

Then she laughs. "You know, Papa, it was strange to see him do the laundry every morning. He pinned the clothes on the line in Mom's upside-down style but ironed in wide sweeps just like you used to. I got such a kick out of watching him iron. It's not my favorite thing, but he seemed to enjoy it."

We are so busy talking, answering each other's questions, that we never realize visiting hours are over until the guard approaches our table and warns us. Quickly, she says goodbye—and promises to return in a few days.

Later on, back in my room, I start to read the second story, "The Devil's Cliff." After the first paragraph, I stop and put it away. I just sit there and rehash the conversation with Doris. Funny how easy it was to talk to her; all the friction of the past is gone. I wonder where she will spend the night. Does she still have friends in our hometown?

The journal—how did she get hold of my journal? Did she bring it with her or did she leave it at home? She did not say much about her family. Maybe it's too soon; maybe she needs more time before she can talk about her loved ones to me.

In the morning, there is a big commotion in the hall, angry screaming, yelled orders, running feet. I'm still a bit dopey, trying to fully wake up, when Otto appears at the door.

"Come on, Griler, get up. I'll help you get dressed. Michael is freaking out. He heard the old priest died last night. Michael is angry—he wanted a full exposure of the dirty deeds. Now it will be all hushed up and nothing will come of the street kids' pain and misery."

"No, Otto. We can't let that happen. Let's talk to Father Lau. There has to be help for the dirty old priest's victims. The church has to make amends for his crimes. This was a chance to get the street kids schooling, training, give them a little hope for the future."

In the afternoon, Otto, Michael, Stephan, and I meet to start brainstorming. We begin listing ideas on how we can spread the truth, get the good citizens of the city to pay attention, bring justice to those who were molested and hurt. They like the little verses I have penned over the last weeks and wonder aloud if they might sound good with modern music. Otto shakes his head. "You know, Griler, rock songs have always celebrated macho power, sexy girls, violence, anger, and untouchable heroes. Do you think songs about the lifelong effects of molestation, sexual violence, physical and mental abuse on its victims, will appeal to the general population?"

Michael chimes in. "What if we get the verses to Toni? The street band he always talks about could give them a try. We need Stephan's friend Ted to organize his buddies on the street. Maybe Ted can also speak to Wiggy's parents, see how they could support our cause—maybe just financially, if they don't want the publicity."

For a moment, I imagine what my verses would sound like in a rap song, accompanied by a street kid playing Wolfgang's old accordion with a vengeance. I burst into laughter. Stephan turns to me. "What's the matter, Griler. You think a street band is funny?"

"No, Stephan, that's not what I find amusing. I just remembered that Toni gave the street band leader the old accordion he found in Mrs. Walters' storage room. I wonder how this antique instrument fits in with a modern band."

They all stare at me and then begin to howl with laughter.

CHAPTER ELEVEN:
The Devil's Cliff

THERE ARE MANY STORIES about the Devil's Cliff. One of them goes like this: A group of monks, living near the river Inn, caught sight of the devil sitting under an oak tree. A short time later, the devil traveled to the Alps. There, he searched for a huge granite boulder, loaded it onto a barge, and floated it up river. He planned to dam the Inn to flood the abbey and drown the monks. When he got back, he stopped to rest and fell asleep. The boat rocked and tipped the granite boulder against the hillside. The devil woke up when the bells in the abbey rang, noticed the boulder leaning against the embankment, kicked it a few times, swore violently, and went straight back to hell.

Wolfgang was on what we called the Artist's Path, which winds its way through the forest higher up. Maybe he thought he was safer up there than on the trail right beside the river. I didn't want to type up all the details, so I condensed his story and turned it into a poem.

THE DEVIL'S CLIFF

nine, maybe ten years ago
late at night, intoxicated
I tottered in the pitch dark
on a narrow, uneven path
tripped on exposed roots
rolled down a slippery slope
scratched my arms and legs
got a nose full of dusty earth

walked back the next day
stared up at the Devil's Cliff
and calculated the distance
from path above to quay
realized a bush saved me
six meters from drowning
in the ice cold river Inn
Thank you, Guardian Angel

attended a jazz concert but
hated the singer's aping of
priests and Catholic symbols
stopped going to church but
still respect religious tenets
late night, on the path again

moonless sky, solid black
blindly prodding my way

my arms reach out, probe
bushes poke, scratch me
tenderly I test my footing
step after step, carefully
too tired to go forward
too far to go back to town
then I see a glimmer of light
from the castle across the Inn

this little beacon in Austria
helps me find my bearings
enables me to see the bench
at the side of the Devil's Cliff
there, I settle down, exhausted
head resting on my back pack
knees pulled up, hands numb
sleep on the wooden slats

I wake up freezing cold
sit up, look around me
limp back onto the path
ground moves, my feet slip
don't look down, stay still
right hand gropes at the earth
then fastens around tree root
left sleeve's soaked in blood

hold on, turn your legs slowly,
the river below me gurgles
shift my right leg, feels fine
left leg throbs as I move it
manage to get on all fours
still grabbing onto tree roots
I grope for rock higher up
inch by inch I crawl upward

curled up on the path above
exhausted, aching but alive
an elderly hiker finds me
examines me, goes for help
brings a blanket, hot coffee
curse you, you Devil's Cliff
tripping me up a second time
Thanks again, Guardian Angel

Once I finish typing, I read my poem aloud, like I used to do. Hearing the words, I feel the rhythm, know if they sound right or need editing. When I look up, I notice Otto standing in the doorway, listening. He seems to be stunned. He has tears in his eyes. "Griler, you are full of surprises. Not only are you a poet, you also know the tale of the Devil's Cliff. There is another story of a boat full of pilgrims capsizing on the way to Maria Hilf Church, all of them drowning not too far from the Devil's Cliff. After this tragedy, the local bishop had a giant cross erected to ward off the devil."

"Sorry to disappoint you, Otto, this is not my story, it's Wolfgang's. Doris dropped off two of his stories a few days ago and I have a hard time dealing with them emotionally. Though Wolfgang obviously fell accidentally, the fact that he behaved recklessly, took stupid risks, angers me. You can't blame it all on his addiction. He is clearly hurting and punishing himself, instead of asking for help."

"You know, Griler, I'm starting to wonder about that daughter of yours. There are rumors going around that she is stirring up a lot of dust by prying into people's affairs. How did she get hold of these stories, anyway? Looks like Wolfgang wrote them years ago. Mrs. Stilz was totally stunned when your daughter gave her the password to Wolfgang's old computer. Her whole team is still laughing about this. **Odd*man53.** No one could have guessed that."

How does this information get to Otto? Here I am, worried about what is happening with my case, and then there are my fellow inmates who know more than I do. Could this be Doris planting ideas, distributing hints and clues, hoping to influence the outcome of the trial? I hope she keeps her word and shows up again before my court date. There are numerous things I need to ask her.

Since our talk and reading Wolfgang's stories, uneasiness is invading my thoughts. The calmness and hopefulness of the past weeks are evaporating. Part of it is my fear of the trial. My gut tells me Doris has a great deal to do with this. Our conversation was all peaceful and friendly. Why do I believe I detected deep-seated anger then? Why did her demeanor remind me of her mother's attitude, just a touch of coldness, not quite rejection, more like a constant annoyance with all I say and do?

When I get paged I head toward the visitors' room filled with trepidation. My hands firmly grab the sidebars on the wheelchair. I try to make myself look strong and ready for a confrontation. Like last time, her greeting is friendly. As I watch her walk toward me and sit down, I realize that she is in pain. The stiff walk, leaning to the right, then carefully straightening her shoulders and shifting to ease pressure on the spine, remind me of my own ailments from my past life.

For once, Doris seems to be struggling for words. After a minute of silence, she looks up at me. "Papa, I talked to numerous people in Rossberg and Arnfeld but I'm not getting anywhere. A shroud of secrecy hovers over anything related to sexual abuse. Shame is still the main motive for silence when there should be loving support to deal with the painful experience of molestation or rape. At this time and age they still hang onto ancient virginity and purity standards for girls and women. It's so sad! Society looks sideways at an innocent child who's been molested instead of exposing the predator and locking them up."

"Doris, are you saying nobody will show up for my hearing?"

"Sorry, Papa! I got carried away with my rant about this culture of secrecy that still exists in small towns."

"That's all right, Doris. You must have inherited that ranting gene from me."

"Looks like it! Remember you gave me Linda's contact information? Her phone was disconnected so I went to the address. The landlady gave me her father's phone number. He called me back but yelled so loud I could not understand what he was saying. Then he just hung up. I think something really bad must have happened to Linda."

This statement forces me to look at my situation from a different angle—the victim's side. I don't have a clue how many children and women Wolfgang hurt. Maybe Doris got ahold of the police reports. I just have to ask. "Do you know how many victims there are and how badly they were hurt?"

She looks at me. "Papa, are you saying that you have no idea what Wolfgang is accused of? You must have seen police reports, heard accusations!"

"No facts, I never saw a piece of paper telling me what Wolfgang did. Everyone expected me, the pedophile, to know that. Sure, I heard hints, faced nasty remarks and insults, but not enough information to figure out what Wolfgang is actually accused of and what is gossip that was spread around after he was caught."

It takes her a moment before she turns to me. "I'll tell you what I know. My first hint was a degenerative remark about Wolfgang from a stranger at the butcher shop. That happened on one of my visits to spend time with Mom. Furtive glances in my direction and a quick response by Maral's mom to shut the speaker up followed.

"Later, I questioned her and she made a vague disclaimer, basically calling the other woman a nasty gossip spreader.

That day was like having a blindfold removed. Suddenly, little flashes of weird moments, things I had picked up and put aside, started to bother me. The love and care I had felt for my little brother was spoiled.

"Each time I went home to see Mom I was distraught about being in the same house. I suddenly noticed odd things about Wolfgang. The rest of the family did not want to talk about him. They blamed his near-death illness at age forty for his marriage failures, lack of ambition, his strange behavior, and growing aggression."

"How about your friends? Won't they tell you what they have heard?"

Doris continues: "Elsa, Olga, and Felix wrote letters because they are friends of mine. Maral is the only one who actually cares about what happens at the trial. That poor woman—I had my suspicions ever since I knew her, but caught on only to half of what she went through. I had no idea that Wolfgang was involved. She kept saying he was only a little boy, maybe three years old, couldn't even talk yet. All I could think of was, why do I not know about this, where was I at that time?"

When I interrupt her with questions about what happened to Wolfgang and Maral, she explains. "Five bullies, about twelve, fourteen, at the time, would corner them while they were playing, then drag them to one of the cow shelters in the fields. They made them strip and prodded and poked them with whatever they felt like. At first, Wolfgang laughed when they pulled down his pants and made him dance and wiggle. When they hurt him, he started to scream and they let them go. The bullies must have bragged about their nasty game because other boys started to assault her, too.

"Oh, Papa, that's when I remembered that Hubert once joked about playing doctor with Maral. Looks like that was anything but playing doctor."

"Doris, he could have been talking about a different time when they were younger. I remember your mom telling me about several children being caught with their pants down. You were banned from playing with Maral and her brother."

"Yes, I remember bits and pieces, but now I have the feeling that Maral was the only innocent one in this doctor-playing game, that she was the victim. She clearly thinks Wolfgang's sexual crimes started with his abuse.

"The first time I came home after your death, my two brothers would not talk to each other. As I prodded them, I found out Wolfgang accused Hubert of always putting him down, making fun of him. There was an incident with a Boy Scout group, I can't remember exactly what, and making him walk from the train station to the school, then driving by with his friends, laughing at him."

When Otto told me about the Boy Scout nightmare in the forest, I had a suspicion that Hubert was involved or at least had heard about it and kept quiet. How much I missed of my children's lives by working out of town after Wolfgang was born. We never had the father-son moments I treasured with Hubert. There was so much to do on my weekends at home. How I dreaded being confronted with all the kids' misdeeds by Erna as soon as I walked in the door.

My daughter's voice brings me back to reality. "You know, it is easy to make excuses and blame his upbringing. As I learned more about sexual perversions, I started to believe that this trait might be inherited and, combined with certain learned behaviors and abuse in early life, that it gets triggered during times of severe depression. Do you recall any ancestors who were known to molest children?"

"The only relative I knew about was an uncle. He was not a blood relative, only the brother of my mother's sister's husband. My cousin Franz and I caught him molesting my other cousin Egon. We were little kids then, the brothers were about nine or ten and I hadn't started school yet. I have no idea if Egon ever spoke up. I do know he left home when he was about fifteen, to live with relatives in Vienna. Also, Max's mother called her first husband a pervert; he would have been your great-grandfather."

"Otto told me that you met your father's spirit in a grey space you think was limbo. That must have been an awesome experience. How about Mom, Hubert, Liz, or Opa and Oma? Did you find their spirits, too?"

"No, Doris, only Liz showed up. Can you believe she was happy there, surrounded by a group of social outcasts, rebels, and free-thinking souls. She couldn't understand why I wanted to leave limbo so badly."

"Papa, Liz was always independent, no wishy-washy emotions for her. You must have been so shocked once you realized whose body you are stuck in and how much trouble awaited you. When I gave Mrs. Stilz the password, I felt it was the right thing to do. Now that I have talked to you, I start having doubts.

"You see, years ago, around the time of the Devil's Cliff story, Wolfgang and I were in regular internet contact. One day, he sent me his password. In case anything happened to him, he wanted me to read his stories. I never did—lack of time and later on a fear of what I might find in them, stopped me."

"Are you saying he wrote about his sexual crimes, provided enough evidence to get himself jailed?"

"No, Papa. I have no idea what he wrote. Once Lucas was born, all his e-mails were about his son. After the stroke, his mental capacities drastically dropped. To this day, I have no idea what actually took place because the stories kept changing. Might have been one of his suicide attempts. Agnes talks so fast that most of the time I could not figure out what she was telling me on the phone."

"Was this after he sold the house and moved to Passau?"

"About three, four years later. Once they moved, Wolfgang no longer had internet access. He blamed computer problems. We communicated only be phone, which is problematic for me. By the way, I read in your army medical report that you were hard of hearing, too. I was hurt that you never told me. Didn't you think it might have been helpful if I could have asked you how you coped at school? Why did you hide it from me?"

"The doctor and your mom decided it would be best for you to live like a normal child. It had nothing to do with me. Darn it, Max's mother was right when she said that I complained and ranted a lot, but never stood up for what I thought was right. Don't ask questions—it's a long story, better told another time."

"OK! My guess is that Wolfgang got caught on a child-porn site and lost his computer privileges."

"You are right, Doris. Lucas said I was banned from the internet, when I asked him how much an old computer would cost. That was right after I arrived at this rehab and was able to start using my left hand a bit."

"Papa, whatever is stored on the old computer, is at least eight years old. The new charges were dropped because it is evident Wolfgang was more or less a victim, not a predator. They are still looking for his fourth wife, Sonja. She will be the one who is responsible for the current child pornography videos. As to the child molestation accusations from the seventies and eighties, few victims are willing to testify now."

Of course I was glad to hear that the evidence against Wolfgang was not as dreadful as I had imagined. In the end, I will have to face a judge and accept whatever the sentence will be and take the punishment. "Well, Doris, I'm willing to go to jail for your brother's crimes, but the guilty plea has to be worded in a way that won't make me a liar."

She nods. "All right, you draft your guilty plea. Then tell Mrs. Stilz when you are ready. You know, Papa, when I read your journal, I experienced moments of understanding, remembered political discussions and our frustrating arguments. Sadly, you wrote the little book you put together for me in shorthand. By the time I got it, I had forgotten what I had learned in middle school for lack for practice."

"All right, I will never write you letters in shorthand again. But, get this, I picked up Wolfgang's English skills and can finally communicate with my grandchildren—that is, if they ever want to talk to me. Being able to hear normally now, I realize how much I misunderstood in my past life. At first these new features frightened me. I worried part of Wolfgang's spirit was still in this body and I might pick up on his bad habits. Just talking with you eliminated a few fears. I'm so glad you came."

"You know, Papa, I have a confession to make. I not only read your journal, I also translated parts of it for my family, including your poems. To pull the different sections of my translated work together, I added a bit of fiction here and there to make it more interesting. Once in a while, I got a bit carried away. I could almost feel you standing behind me, shaking your head."

"Very funny, Doris."

"Next time I see you, I'll give you a copy, and since you can speak English now, you will be able to read it. Feel free to cross things out if they annoy you, edit events and dates you remember differently, and correct my errors. As I got older, I felt an urge to pass on a bit of my heritage and thought I should make up for all the sleepless nights I caused you as a teenager. The fiction part was pure fun. First, I called it my **Dad Project,** but then I thought **The Pathetic Poet** would be a fitting title."

Our Doris is a scribbler like me. I'm stunned. She notices my shocked face. "I never got the writing bug until most of our family had died. While Wolfgang sat on the Vott weir, I put my pain and misery down on paper. Once I signed up for writing classes, I learned to express myself better and developed my own style. Mostly, I write short stories. **The Pathetic Poet** helped me deal with old father-daughter issues."

At this point she looks at her watch and rushes to say goodbye. "A friend is picking me up. I'm staying at her house until the hearing. Remember Rosemarie? She gave you Tommy, your beloved cat."

Doris needs a moment after getting up to find her bearings, then she slowly walks out the door, again leaning to the right, obviously in pain. Why did I not ask her about her health? This omission is so typical in our family. Don't ask unless it is a pleasant subject.

Back in my room, I make notes of important and interesting points in our discussion. It is clear to me that she cares about Wolfgang or she would not be here. Would she have come if I hadn't sent her the letters… if I had not talked to Martin on the phone… if she had not suspected a mysterious connection to me?

The day before the hearing, Mrs. Stilz arrives to go over the procedures and clear any misunderstandings on my part. As soon as I say I intend to plead guilty, she looks at me, a bit spiffed. "Griler, I slaved for months to get a good deal for you and then you decide to plead guilty? At least find out what the final charges are, the ones with enough evidence to get you convicted."

The early morning trip is just a blur caused by the anxiety I feel about facing the judge. Over and over I unfold the piece of paper, read the plea I drafted, and fold the paper carefully again. Reluctantly, I hand it to Mrs. Stilz at our meeting spot. Then I watch in agony as she reads it and crosses out line after line. She reduces my carefully worded plea to just a few sentences.

I sit there terrified and stare at the people moving around me—yet not really seeing anything at all. George, the friendly guard, hands me a bottle of water. "You all right, Griler? Have a sip of water. It will calm you a bit. We only have a few minutes until the hearing starts."

After an explanation of the procedures and an introduction, the hearing starts. Only two accusations will stand: Winter and Bandegger. Suddenly, there is a big commotion behind me and a shrill woman's voice yells: "How dare you leave out my daughter? I want that vile Griler to pay for making my little girl strip and dance. This stupid drunk, liar, filthy piece of shit!"

Next thing, there are running footsteps and the screeching woman is dragged out of the room. As I turn my head, I catch a glimpse of a tall, middle-aged blonde with heavy make-up. Our eyes meet for a second. Now I know who Marianne Kuntz is. When I was young, before I joined the army, I had dated her mother for a few months.

The court clerk asks for quiet and apologizes for the disturbance. "We have a written statement from Mrs. Kuntz's daughter that she has no recall of any contact with the accused, Wolfgang Griler, of any kind and believes that her mother suffers from delusions in this case."

The first victim is a young woman named Michele Bandegger. She explains that she strongly believes society needs to punish molesters. That is the reason she is here. Wolfgang has to pay for what he did to her when she was an innocent child living in the apartment next door to him in Munich. She narrates how he befriended her family and how devastated her mother was when she caught him molesting her child. "I was too young to realize what he did to me was wrong. Yet, we don't know how far he would have gone if my mother had not walked into the room at that moment. She felt so terrible about trusting Wolfgang. We moved away and never saw him again. Then I noticed his name on Twitter and remembered my mother's guilt and pain. I just had to speak up for her."

A Mr. Kurt Winter is called next. The elderly gentleman stands up and reads aloud: "A phone call a few weeks ago set off an avalanche of hurt feeling and painful memories that I had tried hard to suppress. Mr. Griler not only hurt my daughter, he assaulted my granddaughter, too. You see, when my Linda was a child, she was molested by an uncle we all loved. Nobody in the family ever imagined he would molest a child, least of all a dear family member. My Linda was too ashamed to speak up and carried her dirty little secret with her into adulthood. She was a beautiful and smart child and did well in school. That's why I never understood when she started to act out as a teenager.

I mean, she had it all: a loving family, was a successful student, had great friends…"

He wipes his eyes. "We had a suspicion that she was secretly drinking. But then, which teenager does not experiment with alcohol? That's what we told ourselves, her mother and I. It took us a long time to admit that our beloved Linda was an addict. We got help for her. She went to rehab. She fell off the wagon. It became a maddening cycle. Then she had a baby. She loved little Naomi, loved her to bits. Linda tried hard. Had a good job. Kept a neat little apartment. When Naomi was around thirteen years old, Wolfgang came into their life."

Mr. Winter explained that he was charmed by Wolfgang. He seemed to be a nice man, well read, easy to talk to. His only misgivings were that they had met in a support group for former addicts. He feared if one of them failed the other would be dragged down, too. In no way did he imagine that Naomi might get hurt.

"Then one day a sobbing and disheveled Naomi stood at our door screaming at me, **He hurt me… he raped me**. I just took her in my arms and sobbed with her. My wife called Linda and asked her to come over because something terrible had happened to Naomi. That was the worst day in my life. When Linda found out what Wolfgang had done to her daughter, she just freaked out. The secret she had held onto for so many years burst forth. She frantically hit and threw everything in sight."

The police came and an ambulance picked Linda up. The family never fully recovered from that night. Naomi stayed with them. Linda's addiction overtook her despite all attempts to help her turn her life around. Thanks to the best counseling possible, Naomi managed to deal with her trauma. He introduces the young women standing next to him. "This is Naomi. She is a fine young lady and wants other victims to see that one can not only survive but also thrive after a sexual assault."

Total silence fills the room until the court clerk announces the reading of the character witness statements. Just like Doris had guessed, the witness statements praised Erna. The specialist from Munich University Hospital verified that Wolfgang had serious side effects from the experimental treatment he had received to save his life. There was talk about him being a wild child, of possibilities that he might have been abused as a student, the loss of mental capacities, of him sleeping in other people's doorways because he could not find his way home, and about him exposing himself in his drunken stupor. Then there was the other side: glowing reports about the new Wolfgang, who was kind and understanding, who was a totally different person according to my new friends, the staff at the rehab center, Father Kamau, and Father Lau.

Finally, the moment I have been dreading, and in some ways eagerly waiting for, arrives. With George's assistance, I manage to stand up to read my guilty plea. Then I face the victims. "I'm so glad you had the strength to stand up in court. I apologize for the physical and mental pain I caused you. I'm so sorry."

The judge seems to be glad that he does not have to deal with the **Wolfgang versus Joseph change of person** issue. As George wheels me out, I look among the rows of seats for Doris. All the faces look solemn, nobody stares at me except Maral. My daughter has an eerie, satisfied smile on her face. Mrs. Stiltz shakes my hand without saying a word. When I look back over my shoulder, Doris is gone from her seat.

CHAPTER TWELVE:
Down Memory Lane

BACK AT THE REHAB, I find a letter on my bed. I rip it open immediately. Mrs. Walters wrote:

Dear Joseph,

I hope you don't mind me being on first-name basis, but it seemed silly to call you Mr. Griler. This daughter of yours certainly knows how to push buttons. Her inquiries disturbed a few conservative minds. Our conversations were mind boggling, since I never expected to discuss sexual perversions and methods of treatment at the age of eighty-six. To hear Doris and Toni speak about the legal implications of chemical and surgical castration of pedophiles, banning them to deserted *islands or locking them up for life, was a bit frightening.*

There is one thing I have to say though, she had a wonderful influence on Toni. Being with her calms him and he is turning into a nice young man. Joseph, I have kept your stuff in my storage area and there will always be a bed for you at my place after your release until you get settled.

Sincerely, Else Walters

I'm delighted because this is the first time I have been called Joseph since I landed back on earth and I'm relieved by her promise of a place to stay after I serve my sentence.

The next day, I keep myself busy with typing, in order to avoid talking about the hearing and to stop myself from stressing about the future. I have never been inside a jail—how will I manage as a handicapped person? Where did Doris go? There is a possibility that she is already on the way home, her mission accomplished. Why else has she not come to see me?

Two days later, early in the morning, George comes around. "Get up, Griler, and dress quickly. You have an appointment. We'll leave in twenty minutes."

Like clockwork, George appears at the appointed time, wheels me down the hall, out the gate, and toward a black van. The driver opens the back door and lets down a ramp. George pushes me up and into the van. I hear a giggle and then the words, "Good morning, Papa. I managed to talk the judge into letting me take you on a field trip. George will come with us for security reasons. The driver is a guard, too.

"You've had a tough time since you landed back on Earth. The least I can do is take you on a trip down memory lane. Look out the window, the driver is giving you a special tour of downtown Passau. Then we head toward Rossberg on the old back roads where we used to ride our bikes with you."

Fascinated, I stare out the window. I recognize buildings on a side street. Most of the Dome is hidden underneath scaffolding. We drive under the overhead walk of the seminary I attended a century ago on bumpy, cobbled streets. The road leading to the train station is barely recognizable. Apartment buildings and shopping malls have replaced the narrow townhouses I remember. At this point I lose my bearing until I see the Danube and the castle on the hill. Within minutes, we enter the autobahn leading out of town, but turn off again at the first exit.

Slowly, the van travels down old roads, past small hamlets and farms I have seen a hundred times. I'm too excited to talk and just point out buildings and areas that have a special meaning to me. As we approach my hometown, my eyes search for the church steeple sticking out over the hill. After the **Entering Rossberg** sign, Main Street looks pretty much the way I remember it. The van drives past the church, turns into our street, and parks across from our house... that is no longer ours.

George pushes me out of the van and for a minute I feel like I've entered another time zone. Here I am back in a wheelchair on the street that I rode up and down numerous times in the last decade of my former life. Doris is quiet, too. Like Ms. Meindl told me, the property is well kept, but the yard looks bland without Erna's beautiful garden. The bright begonias hanging from the balcony, the pink phlox along the fence, and the beautiful rosebushes are missing. Then the absence of our huge pear tree hits me. "Oh, no, our pear tree was cut down."

Doris explains, "The city wanted to get rid of that tree for years, because the pears made such a mess in the parking lot. Mom refused and they could not go against her wishes. The tree was part of the contract when Opa sold the property to the city as part of the new soccer field. Wolfgang told me it was cut down two days after Mom died, they didn't even wait until after the funeral."

We head toward the cemetery. I ask George to go slowly so I can read the names on the gravestones as he pushes the wheelchair toward the family plot. Our grave looks plain compared to the ones next to it, most likely because the new graves have elaborate stones.

Doris narrates the grave payment dilemma. "Papa, Helga paid for the grave after Mom died, but she can no longer drive down several times a year. She wants to cancel the lease and asked me to make the arrangements. That's how I met Father Kamau. Then I found out the grave is in Wolfgang's name, so I can't cancel the contract."

George stares at me. "Griler, doesn't it feel strange to stand at your own gravesite? There can't be many people who had that experience before you."

At this point, I'm closer to tears than laughter. He stops when he takes a look at my sad face. Confusion starts to build up in my mind. "Wolfgang's name should be on the stone, not mine."

Doris looks at me seriously. "You know, I thought about that, too, but there is no doubt that your body is buried in the grave and Wolfgang's is standing here. In my opinion, graves are for bodies, not souls.

"Since I have not been to any family funerals, I felt a bit guilty and paid the fees. The rough-edged, grey stone looks shabby and the lettering is barely readable. What do you think? Should we get the letters repainted or buy a brand new stone?"

"Don't worry about the grave. My friend Otto is an artist. He will touch up the names, I think gold would look better than the black lettering. Say thanks to Helga for taking care of our family plot. I will look after it from now on."

"In that case, Papa, let's move on. We started out with the most difficult and emotional part of your field trip—let's head back to the van and continue our ride down memory lane. Which direction would you like to take?"

I can't explain why, but I want them to drive toward the river Rott. We stop at an old bridge. While I stare up river at my favorite swimming spot, Doris tells me, "Wow, Papa, you picked a spot of my childhood nightmares. How scared I was each time you made me walk across the Rott, below the dam with the water cascading in an arc over us."

Surprised, I look at her. Was she really that frightened? My intent was to help her get over being such a chicken. She was the oldest and freaked out about everything. Now in hindsight, I know you can't make people brave by scaring them. Doris spent ten years in my mother's care, witnessing her hysterical fits on a regular basis. A bit of that craziness rubbed off on the child. I understood that, but tried to fix it the wrong way.

She grins when I apologize for being mean to her. "It's OK. I got past it."

After a while, we cross over the one-lane, covered wooden bridge. It is older than I am and survived two World Wars. A little further ahead is the farm where my mother worked from age ten to fifteen. I point this fact of our family history out to Doris.

Next, we enter the village Arnfeld, where I lived during my elementary school years. Doris asks the driver to turn right. "Papa, I would love to take you for lunch across the border to Austria, but it's too risky because you don't have an identity card. George and the driver made that clear to me. We'll stop at the parking lot at the border and push you in the wheelchair along the river."

To my surprise, George heads onto the bridge, then stops halfway to give me a chance to look aground. I ask him to help me up, so I can lean against the railing and get a better look. On the Austrian side, I sees the quay leading to a famous spa and the path to my cousin's house.

Slowly, they push me down the street as I stare across the Inn at Schatting and let myself be overwhelmed with old memories.

While I show George and Doris the house I used to live in as a little boy, the van drives up and we get in. How well I remember huffing and puffing up this steep hill as a child. At the intersection, where my old school stands, we turn left and head south. Doris says: "There is a nice restaurant with a beautiful view of Schatting. We are early enough to get a good seat and the food is pretty good. I have been there with my classmates. Look over there, that's our old doctor's place and here is the drugstore, remember?"

A few minutes later, we are seated near a window, the riverfront of the quaint medieval town Schatting before us and the soft hills of Upper Austria in the background. Doris points below us, a bit to the south, at the soccer field. "There it is, Hubert's place of glory as a soccer player and my spot of embarrassment each year on sports day. The only sport I was ever good at was dodgeball. I think I was born clumsy and old age just makes it worse."

When I ask Doris what's wrong with her, she shakes her head. "There is no proper diagnosis, the doctors ruled out Multiple Sclerosis, but the symptoms I experience are similar to what you went through in your sixties?"

I suggest we talk about pleasant, positive things on this field trip.

"Papa, there is one more thing I need to tell you first. When I spoke with Mrs. Stilz, she told me the average sentence for the child molestation charges you pleaded guilty to is two to three years. The maximum would be five. The judge agreed to let you serve your time in the rehab center instead of moving you to a jail because of your physical disabilities and thanks to your perfect record there. The staff spoke highly of you. The eight months you spent there will be deducted from your sentence."

I let out a sigh of relief. This information relaxes me and I start to truly enjoy myself. Mostly, we chat about old times, things we both experienced. The food is delicious, a bit spicier than I was used to, but really fresh and flavorful. I had no idea I would enjoy a meal that much, and even had a light beer, with George's approval.

The moment we push away our plates, an elderly gentleman approaches and asks if we are Grilers from Rossberg. His mother would like to talk to us. The Brucker name seems familiar. Before I have a chance to say anything, Doris replies, "Sorry, we are tourists."

When I ask her why she lied, she looks a bit embarrassed. "Papa, I did not want him to remember me. My friends and I had a crush on him and his friends when we went to middle school. All three rode silver Vespas. We kind of made fools of ourselves trying to get their attention."

Then she explains that Mrs. Brucker recognized her because she used to bring Erna to their salon for haircuts. Since the subject of Erna has come up, I start asking questions about her. Like Max told me, Doris also thought her mother was fine, just a bit lonely. After her heart valve operation, she slowed down quite a bit, complained about leg pains, had a consistent, dry cough, and was a bit off balance. They hid her bike to prevent accidents. That reduced Erna's independence, especially her shopping trips.

"You know, Papa, I'm glad I spent nearly all my holidays with her from the year after you died until she passed away. This was a new mom, none of the friction of the past surfaced, we talked and giggled and did things together. The first time I came back after her recovery from the aneurysm, she had no idea who I was. On the second day, she woke me up early and sent me to the baker for fresh buns, as if I was still ten years old.

She worked in the garden, but was afraid to bend over and get dizzy. When she came in, she had a nap, then another one after lunch.

I used to lie down in the afternoon to rest my back. She'd come in the room, snuggle up to me, and tell me story after story from her childhood, of the happy moments in her life. By that time, she had stopped cooking, since everything tasted funny, as she said. I tried putting bigger labels on the spice jars, but she still got them mixed up. Then one day, I came home after I visited a friend and the house smelled of plum cake. We were a bit scared to take the first bite, but it tasted delicious."

"Why did you go home every year after my death? You ignored me, though I begged you repeatedly to come home."

"Well, Papa, I had health problems that made flying impossible. The year you died, I had the operation I needed. In the late eighties, I faced serious struggles, at work and with the kids. I'm glad you asked though—I felt bad about not visiting you for so many years.

"Let's get back on our field trip. We still have one last stop to look forward to."

Again, we avoid the freeway and take an old road, winding its way through small hamlets. When we approach Altweg, I get all excited, but before I can say anything, Doris instructs the driver to turn off toward the castle. We stop for a moment at the gate to the castle park, while Doris shows the guard the narrow road she would like to go down. He nods and, a few minutes later, we reach the place where my birth house once stood.

The house where I was born is gone. A huge pillar stands in that corner. George explains that the new bridge is called **Friendship Bridge**, bringing the citizens on both sides of the river Inn closer together. He pushes the wheelchair onto the bridge and I enjoy the beautiful view. On the right, a bit farther down, the Devil's Cliff looms darkly. Below it, the large gilded cross gleams in the afternoon sun.

Our final stop is the café across from the castle, where Otto is waiting for us, sitting on a table by the window and waving us over. Doris says: "You know, Papa, I dreaded the moment of saying goodbye, so I asked Otto to come, hoping to lighten the mood. We'll have coffee and cake for your sweet tooth, and enjoy an uplifting conversation. That's how I want to remember you."

We start with politics and the environment before we hit the subject that is really on our minds. Where was my soul for twenty-eight years and how long will I be able to stick around in Wolfgang's body? Otto sort of accepts the idea of a limbo as a grey area, for people who are undecided or, as Max said, sitting on the fence. All of us, except the guard who keeps himself out of our discussion, have problems with Max's travel-to-Earth stories, about his soul merging with animal bodies.

Incarnation plays a big part in Christianity. Mary's conception of Jesus is the incarnation of God's son into a human being. In medieval stories, incarnation was mainly about the devil possessing animals. That I managed to target my own son's body at the moment of Wolfgang's suicide seems too far stretched to accept, even for modern, liberal minds. What would have happened to my spirit if the doctors had not managed to resuscitate Wolfgang's body? Neither one of us has an answer to these questions.

Doris points out that there are many cultures who believe in animism. Reincarnation plays a big role in the Hindu religion, but the soul enters an animal body before birth. To be reborn as a rat is considered punishment for bad deeds in the previous life. Then she jokes: "See that sparrow on the tree branch there? That could be a relative of ours, watching over us, or our worst enemy, waiting to attack."

As I stare at the sparrow, I think I can hear a tweet and get all excited. "I can hear it tweet through the window. I don't believe this, I can hear a bird tweet, I really can."

"What's the big deal, Griler? All of us can hear birds tweet," laughs George.

Doris stares at me before she corrects him. "No, George, not all of us. I can't hear it and Papa couldn't either in his former life. He got Wolfgang's hearing now."

There is a moment of silence, then we talk about moments in our life when an animal felt extra special to us. Doris remembers a little goat she got emotionally attached to and her grief when it disappeared. George tells us about his dog Treffi, who has soulful brown eyes and is his most trustworthy friend. Then we graduate to stories about animals who attacked for no reason whatsoever, as if they carried an old grudge toward the victim.

Otto thinks there may be a simpler explanation to my resurrection. Considering new scientific experiments with genes, would it not be possible that parts of our spirits or our souls are in these genes and get passed on from one generation to the next one?

"Well, Otto, this would mean trouble for children who come from families who hate each other. Wouldn't those genes fight over control of the grey cells in our brain? I can just see the Prussians and the Bavarians battling in my head," is George's comment.

Even the guard joins our laughter.

" A few weeks ago, I read an article about a new alternative trend called somatic archaeology, where they try to uncover ancestral pain in living bodies. Apparently, we did not only inherit the DNA of our ancestors but also pain and traumas they experienced. During the treatment they try to identify the seed of the pain and trace it back to its origin. The article claimed success in treating Holocaust survivors, veterans, and patients suffering anxiety attacks.

"Therapists lead the patients to analyze behavior and learning processes that have been passed on for generations. They were useful at the time they originated, but are hindering spiritual growth now. Dreadful experiences are often suppressed and stored in the unconscious, then carried forward for generations, either out of habit or respect for the people who taught us. The article calls this 'historical amnesia.' Well, Doris, maybe that is the cause of the physical pain we suffer, centuries of hard labor, starvation, mistreatment, even torture of lowest-class peons."

"You know, this is not all that new to me. Our Liz strongly believed that learned behavior and knowledge are important, but inherited spiritual knowledge can work against our efforts to improve our life. We were in our twenties at the time and I did not take her seriously."

Our group is split on this issue. Despite his own struggles as an addict, Otto strongly believes that we all have the ability to change. Doris jokes, "In that case, we all have hope for the future. Papa could become the writer he always wanted to be. Otto could renascence his art career. George, what did you dreamed of becoming?"

Otto laughs. "Griler, now I understand why you were so worried about her. She must have been the most recalcitrant child to raise. Looks like women in Canada are quite liberal in their thinking—or are you a rare specimen?"

"You can't help being open-minded living among so many different cultures. There are people who keep saying that integration does not work. I think it depends on where you come from. Hong Kong immigrants came for financial reasons and out of fear that China would take them over. They arrived in the late nineties and have not adapted themselves to our culture, they hang onto their own language. Normally, the second generation born in Canada feels Canadian."

Again, Otto laughs. "Do any of you even know what a real Canadian is? Wouldn't you have to be Aboriginal then?"

"Come on, Otto. To be German does not mean you wear Lederhosen, drink beer from a stein, and eat only sauerkraut and sausages. Not every Norwegian is a true Viking."

As I watch those two sparring, it occurs to me that they are well-matched in their liberal opinions. Too bad Doris is leaving. She must have watched my face because she turns to me and, as if she had guessed my thoughts, she warns me. "Papa, you have that match-making expression on your face. Remember how badly you fared with that Austrian suitor you chose for me? I'm over seventy now and such thoughts are totally wasted in my case. Let's not spoil this lively discussion."

Otto chimes in. "Griler, do you realize your daughter is older than you now and at this stage, all fatherly advice is basically redundant?"

Now, this is a turn of events all right—the two oldest at our table putting me in my place. Seeing my unease, Doris says: "Honestly, Papa, we are just kidding. I'm proud of you. In a short time, you have rejuvenated Wolfgang's mind and body, erased years of abuse. Do your exercises and keep your mind occupied, so our ancestors' traumas don't have a chance to affect you. There is a bright future ahead for all open-minded people."

George and the guard remind us that we have to head back to rehab. As I turn around, Doris is gone. Frantically, I ask Otto where she went. He points to the door. A moment later, she reappears with a large bag and walks back to our table. First, she hands me my journal, then the little booklet I had written for her (with a sticker on it that says: return to sender, undecipherable) and what she calls her manuscript of **The Pathetic Poet.**

My hand automatically reaches for the journal, caresses the cover. For the first time, I can actually touch an object of my past life. This is not some sentimental trinket. This journal contains my writing, my dreams, my personal life experiences, dating from my teenage years to a few days before my death.

Doris puts the other things back in the bag and hands it to George. "There are letter-size envelopes, paper, and stamps good for the weight of ten pages to Canada. I hope Papa will work on his biography and sends me draft copies once in a while."

"Thank you all for this lovely afternoon. I truly enjoyed our conversation and, if everything works out, we will continue our discussion in two or three years. Now, Papa, I'm not good at saying goodbyes. Rosemarie is waiting for me in the car. She will take me to the airport tomorrow. Remember, today we took a trip down memory lane. Now we are starting a new chapter."

She raises her water bottle. "To new friendships and resurrected fathers!"

Then Doris gives me a hug and walks away. At the door she stops and turns back. "Ah, Papa, just in case you end up in the grey area before I see you again, say **Hello** to Max and Liz from me."

Otto is shaking with laughter. "Nice parting shot, Griler."

We say goodbye and he promises to visit me soon. George pushes me outside.

The air is cool. A gentle wind blows from the east.

As we get in the van, the church bells ring and out of habit I count along: six rings means six o'clock. I'm exhausted from the outing and feel a tinge of sadness that Doris is gone.

Carefully, my fingers flip through the pages of my beloved journal and gently touch the words I wrote so many years ago.

Our field trip down memory lane released century-old guilt, resentments, and worries. The whole day was filled with delights. My heart is overstimulated from the excitement of retrieving bits and pieces of my former life and my head is spinning from the interesting conversations I took part in.

Leaning back in the wheelchair, I close my eyes. I'm blissfully happy and, for the first time, I feel comfortable in Wolfgang's body.

Printed in Canada